## ABOUT THIS BOOK

From *USA Today* bestselling author Valia Lind—She goes on a hunt for answers, only to discover what she never realized she wanted until now.

Niccola knows two things: her mother has disappeared and she needs to find her long-lost father.

By some providence, Niccola ends up in Colorado, with nothing but a backpack. When she arrives at the small town of Havenwood Falls in the Rocky Mountains, she quickly realizes that her family's history is much more complicated than she ever knew. She's no stranger to keeping secrets, but even she's not prepared for what she finds.

While Niccola tries to unravel her past, she meets a gorgeous deputy-in-training who could be her future. She's spent her whole life protecting her secret, because being a half witch, half shifter is not something that goes over well with her coven. Yet, Warren sees past the labels and straight into her heart. She doesn't believe in destiny, but maybe she needs to rethink that.

Together, they must do whatever it takes to find the truth and save her mother. Time is running out, and Niccola must find it in herself to trust the town and its people, or lose it all forever.

# PREDESTINED

## A HAVENWOOD FALLS HIGH NOVELLA

VALIA LIND

# HAVENWOOD FALLS HIGH BOOKS

*Written in the Stars* by Kallie Ross

*Reawakened* by Morgan Wylie

*The Fall* by Kristen Yard

*Somewhere Within* by Amy Hale

*Awaken the Soul* by Michele G. Miller

*Bound by Shadows* by Cameo Renae

*Inamorata* by Randi Cooley Wilson

*Fata Morgana* by E.J. Fechenda

*Forever Emeline* by Katie M. John

*Reclamation* by AnnaLisa Grant

*Avenoir* by Daniele Lanzarotta

*Avenge the Heart* by Michele G. Miller

*Curse the Night* by R.K. Ryals

*Blood & Iron* by Amy Hale

*Shadows & Spells* by Cameo Renae

*Falling Deep* by J.L. Weil

*Saving Infiniti* by Rose Garcia

*Willful* by Liz Ferry

*Cast in Moonlight* by Ali Winters

*Promise the Moon* by Kallie Ross

*Blurred Lines* by Daniele Lanzarotta

*Ascending Darkness* by J.L. Weil

*Finding Infiniti* by Rose Garcia

*Unicorn's Lament* by Megan Linski

*Paper Bird* by Amy Richie

*Predestined* by Valia Lind

*Rediscovered* by Morgan Wylie

Stay up to date at www.HavenwoodFalls.com

Subscribe to our reader group and receive free stories and more!

# BOOKS BY VALIA LIND

*For Mom, my greatest inspiration for the kind of a person I strive to be*

# CHAPTER 1

*Find your father.*

For the hundredth time, I stare at the piece of paper with my mother's handwriting and the three simple words that shatter every notion I've ever had. I thought my mother hated him. I've hated him my whole life. Now I have to find him?

My mother's magic is all over the paper, but I can't tell if it's meant to help me or just residual from whatever happened here. We were supposed to go to dinner together. I ran out to pick up mail from our PO box and came back to my whole life ruined.

Looking up, I glance around the disarray that is our living room. The apartment is small, but we've lived here long enough to collect all kinds of keepsakes. Which are now thrown all over the area.

The panic I felt when I first walked through the open door hasn't really subsided. But Mom has taught me how to control it—and my magic—enough that I can keep a clear mind.

Whatever happened here, she's in trouble, and I have no choice but to follow the clues she left. Which is why I don't call the police or the coven. Instead, I walk over to her room, picking up a few discarded items, then I settle myself in front of our coffee table. After I flip it over back on its feet.

Next I light a candle, then I place my phone facing up in front of me. It's the closest thing I have to a black mirror, and I need it to scry. I pull my necklace over my head, the small quartz crystal dangling on the bottom. It's all I've got.

Holding the crystal in my hand, I close my eyes and set an intention. When I open my eyes, I place a tip of my finger against the phone, and ask for my mother's location. My body buzzes with magic, heating the crystal I'm holding. Leaning in, I look closely, studying the fuzzy image appearing on the surface of the phone.

But it's gone before I can make out too much of it.

"Come on," I whisper under my breath, as I try to force myself to stay calm and focused. The crystal heats up again, a town's name coming into focus before it's gone again.

"Denver?" I mumble, incredibly confused and a bit frustrated. This isn't giving me much information. When I try the third time, I end up with nothing but some mountains in the distance.

"This is useless!" I snap, sending some of my unchecked magic at the candle and throwing it against the opposite wall. Thankfully, the flame goes out, or I would be in so much trouble.

But that brings me to the problem at hand. I can't be in trouble, because my mother is not here to declare I'm in trouble. My chest grows heavy, and I try to keep my breathing centered.

"Think, Nic. You got this," I say out loud, just to hear a voice. Reaching for my phone, I open a browser and type in Denver, followed by mountains.

"Denver, Colorado? What the heck is in Colorado?" As far as I know, my mother has never been to Colorado. Or anywhere near it. I spent my whole life between California and Nevada. But if there is one thing she has taught me, it's to trust my magic. So that's what I'm going to do.

I walk over to my room, pulling out my backpack and stuffing three changes of clothes into it. After grabbing a toothbrush and paste, I search for my favorite lotion but can't find it anywhere. My body moves on autopilot, reaching for what I need, but my mind is completely on my mother.

What did she get herself into?

She's been acting weird for weeks now, but she wouldn't exactly share what was going on. Maybe I should've pushed harder and tried to figure it out. But I'm only seventeen. It's not like she was going to trust me with a huge problem, no matter how close we are. She's still my mother, and she will do anything to protect me. Of that, I have no doubt.

But she's gone now. And it's my turn to do the protecting.

Determination fuels my every move as I do another sweep of the apartment. Satisfied that I have everything I'll need for the trip, I swing the backpack over my shoulder and walk out of my room.

One last long look at the mess of our apartment, and I'm out the door. It's no time to be sentimental, or to let the feelings creep in. If I break down, there's no going back. I have enough problems as it is. Like figuring out how I'm going to survive a plane ride, since I hate flying.

It doesn't take me long to land in Colorado, but it's way longer than I'm comfortable with. Surprisingly, I got a flight out in just a few hours. Even though I tried, I couldn't sleep on the plane. My body is in constant hyperawareness; every person I meet is a possible threat.

With my backpack slung over my shoulder, I step outside the airport doors, trying to think of my next move. My eyes are instantly drawn to a pair of vans parked at the curb. They're nothing special, standard-issue passenger vans, except for the gorgeous images wrapped all around the body of the vehicle. Before I realize what I'm doing, I've taken a few steps toward the vans.

I freeze in my tracks, confused by this sudden pull toward the vans and the town painted on the doors. It's not like I'm sentimental about outdoorsy places, or unknown towns in a state I've never been in, so the only explanation must be magic. My mom taught me to trust my instincts, and my instincts are telling me to get in the van.

"Looking for something?" The deep raspy voice reaches me before the man walks around the front of the van. Dressed in a flannel shirt, jeans, and a leather coat that is much warmer than my own, he looks like what I would imagine my grandfather would look like. If I had one.

"A ride?" I don't sound sure of myself, so I clear my throat and try again. "A ride please. To . . ." I wave my hand toward the van's décor, and the man smiles.

"It would be my pleasure."

For someone who doesn't trust people, I find myself completely okay getting in the van with this stranger. I'm not the only one. A few people get in after me. I can tell they're human right away, dressed to go skiing, so I move to the back, keeping my eyes on them and the driver.

My hand reaches into my pocket to make sure my mom's note is still in there. I find instant comfort the moment I touch it. It's like a part of her is with me. For just a second, I let myself feel. The worry, anger, and emotions all rush in at once, and I have to keep myself from audibly gasping. Tears well up in my eyes, but I'm done feeling sorry for my situation, so I push them back. Along with the feelings. The only thing that's left is determination.

Maybe I should be more scared. Maybe I should be a crying mess on the floor. But my mom raised me to take care of myself, and a part of me thinks she's been preparing me for this exact moment. I may only be seventeen, but I'm no weakling. I will do whatever it takes to find my mother. Even if that means finding the man who abandoned us before I was even born.

# CHAPTER 2

*I* blink my eyes a few times, completely lost in my thoughts, when I see a sign flash by as we drive. I'm so out of it, the six-hour drive just flew by.

*Welcome to Havenwood Falls.*

Can't say I've ever heard of the town, but then again, I don't know everything there is to know about Colorado. The people in front of me are chatting away, but all I can do is stare at the passing trees. I don't even know what I'm doing here. Once I get to town, I'll need to do another spell to try to get myself out of this mess.

A few miles down the road, the town opens up below us. It looks like something out of a movie. I think that even more once we pull up at the inn. Everyone piles out, so I have no choice but to follow. The crisp late autumn air and the altitude hit me at once, and I pull my jacket tighter around me. I'll probably need to invest in something warmer if I'm to stay any length of time.

"I hope you find what you are looking for," the old man says as I reach to give him cash for the ride. "This one is on me." He smiles warmly, and for some reason, I think he knows more than he's saying. But before I have a chance to ask, he's talking to someone else, and I'm on my own once again.

I study the building in front of me, Whisper Falls Inn. The name is a bit strange, considering. Shouldn't that say Havenwood Falls Inn? Shrugging, I study the three story Victorian-style manor. It's gorgeous. Like something out of a gothic novel. A Christmas garland, red bows, and lights adorn the exterior. From where I'm standing, I can see a large tree in the front window. If I had my camera with me, I'd probably walk around the property and take some pictures. But that's not why I'm here.

Instead of going inside, I turn my back to the door. Right in front of me is what I can only call the town square. It's like this town stepped right off the front of a postcard. I shake my head as I start walking. The decorations are everywhere. Even the lampposts are sporting garlands and bows. My eyes are drawn to the large gazebo off to the side, with its lights and Christmas decor. When I look closer, I notice a few sun symbols and decorations, which makes me think someone here celebrates Yule. Snow blankets the area around me, completing that magical small-town look.

School must be out for break, because even though it's early afternoon, there are kids and teenagers everywhere. Thankfully, that means I don't stand out. As I walk, I can't help but feel like I belong here. I'm not what my coven calls a reader witch, so I'm not as in tune with emotions, but I do have a few reader talents.

With my own magic, I can decipher humans from supes pretty easily, and I can tell this town is full of both. But I don't know how many of them are friendlies. I have to tread carefully. Glancing up, I see that I'm on Main Street. This seems like a perfect place to start, so I decide to head away from the inn.

The town square is surrounded by businesses on every side, each decorated for the holidays. From what I can see, there's everything from a music store to a pawn shop to a coffee shop. My stomach growls the moment my eyes land on Coffee Haven, and I realize it's been a while since I've had anything to eat.

When I step inside the cafe, the smell of coffee is instantly welcoming. But there's also an undercurrent of something otherworldly here. My eyes scan the area, landing on a few strategically placed crystals, pine cones, and candles. I smile to myself. Someone here definitely loves Yule. I bet norms eat this atmosphere up. But I'd be lying if I said I didn't enjoy it myself. It's nice to know there is someone like me here. Even though I'm not about to broadcast it.

"Hi. What can I get you?" The woman behind the counter is a few years older than me, with silvery hair and the most beautiful bluish eyes I've ever seen. Her voice is soft, and she seems friendly enough. I can absolutely see her as the one who placed all the crystals around the place.

"Hi. Could I get a caramel coffee and one of those blueberry scones, please?" I glance down at her name tag: Willow. She gives me a smile before ringing up my order, and I hand over the cash. The exchange makes me a bit apprehensive, since I have a very limited supply of money at the moment. Getting that flight to Denver took more of my savings than I would've liked. With that worry, all the others rush in. The only reason I would be drawn to this town had to be because somehow it would help. But I have no idea where to start, and the panic starts to set in.

Willow's demeanor changes just enough that I know she must've seen something in my eyes. Even though her customer-friendly smile hasn't left her face, she's studying me carefully. With a quick thanks, I grab my order and move to one of the tables. But I can still feel her eyes on me. Clearly, I need to be even more careful about keeping my demeanor neutral. Maybe they just don't trust outsiders. If there's a magical community here, I can understand that all too well.

It takes me five minutes to eat my snack, and then I'm up and out. A part of me wants to march back in there and demand answers. But I doubt Willow knows about my father or what happened to my mom. She might have her own reasons to be suspicious. I shake my head again, trying to keep the panic at bay. I need to shut it all down. I can't afford emotions right now.

When I leave the cafe, I just walk, looking for some kind of a clue as to why I was led here. I probably should've seen if there was a room at the inn before I decided to explore, but it's too late now.

When I stop in front of the old red three-story building, all thoughts of cold and homelessness are forgotten. There's something curious about the building, and when I look over at the sign, I read it out loud.

"Havenwood Falls High."

Of course a small town would have one of these movie-esque high schools, and something inside of me twinges at the idea of attending one. But this isn't why I'm here, and once the fascination subsides, the frustration sets in.

After taking a deep breath, I pull out my necklace and Mom's note, closing my eyes in concentration. My magic sparks as I try to see past what's here. I don't even know why I'm doing this, except that it seems like a locator spell would be a good idea. But after a few tries, there's nothing.

"Now what?" I ask out loud, wishing my mother were here to help.

"Now I think you should answer some questions."

I spin around at the voice, coming face to face with a gorgeous dark-haired guy. He seems to be a few years older, and definitely a few inches taller, than me. His dark blue eyes are narrowed as he studies me in turn. He's wearing jeans and a dark-colored shirt with no jacket.

"Excuse me?" I finally seem to find my voice. "Did you need something?"

Maybe I'm being a little rude, but the way he's watching me is making me uncomfortable. I've never had to use my battle magic as of yet, but my mom has taught me, just in case. There's something about him that's putting me on edge.

"As I stated previously, you need to answer some questions."

"And what questions might those be?" I ask, but for some unbelievable reason, I calm my magic.

"What brings you to Havenwood Falls?"

"Are you the Havenwood Falls police? Am I not allowed to be here?" He may be gorgeous, but he sounds like he's lost his mind. I reach out with my intuitive magic, and I can tell he's a supe too. I just can't pinpoint which kind. Not a witch, that much I can tell.

"I am the police." His voice shocks me back to present. "And

8

you're allowed to be here, but you've set off some alarms that need to be discussed."

"I'm going to need you to explain yourself, because you're not making any sense."

Now I am being a bit rude, but I don't have time for this. I should've guessed he was police though. He carries himself with some authority.

"State your business, please."

That's how we're going to play this? I'm getting more irritated by the minute. Since some part of me has decided he poses no physical threat to me, my magic has gone dormant. But the other side of me—the attitude side, as my mother likes to call it—is all fired up.

"How about you state your business, Mr. Officer? I don't seem to be breaking any laws." I wave my hands around myself. His eyes narrow once more, and I wonder if that's just his regular state of being. The smell of burgers drifts over to me as a couple opens a door to a restaurant on the other side of the street.

"You came to town on a mission."

"Maybe I just like small towns during the holidays." I shrug as he narrows his eyes once more. As I study him, my magic flares up, and I have no idea if it's because of how tired I am or if it's because of the guy standing in front of me. I'm annoyed at him, but there's something that I can almost call a pull to him, and I don't get it. Knowing I'm not going to be liked for this, I ask anyway, "What are you?"

"What?" His whole body goes rigid in a split second, and it seems like he's grown a few inches. The growl that emanates from somewhere deep gives me an answer I'm looking for.

"A shifter, then," I say, smiling a little, because that explains a lot.

"How do you . . ."

"I'm not exactly human myself," I say, rolling my eyes. His own dart around the area, as if he's making sure no one heard us. I was right to assume they have a tight-knit magical community, and by the way he's acting, the humans know nothing about it. He hasn't relaxed with my proclamation, which means I'm really not handling this well.

"Look, my mom has gone missing. I think something or someone took her. The only clue I found was her telling me to find my father. When I did a scrying spell, it led me to Colorado. I have no idea what possessed me to get on the shuttle, but here I am. Explain that."

I hand the piece of paper to him like a peace offering, and after a moment's hesitation, he takes it. After reading over it, he meets my eyes once more.

"I'm sorry to hear that." He sounds like he means it.

I look away toward the shopping center and the people milling around. The last few days seem to be catching up with me, and this shifter's scrutiny is not helping.

"This is how the town works," he continues, and this time his voice is a little softer. Maybe he's picking up on my mood, and I really need to reel it in, before I become a blabbering mess.

"Okay, cool. I'd love to hear all about it, but I'm tired, and I probably should find a place to sleep tonight."

"I should really take you to meet the sheriff first. He'll go over the rules with you and . . ."

"Listen, I'm not stupid. I'm not going to walk around using my powers."

That stops him. "You have . . ."

"Powers. Yes." I shake my head at the shifter, wondering if everyone is this cagey and suspicious around here. "I've had them since I was five. I know how to keep a secret."

"That's young."

"Yes, thank you for that, shifter."

He growls again, his eyes once more on the people in our vicinity. I almost laugh out loud, but I know not to push shifters too far. I also know how close you have to be to overhear something, and none of the humans are that close. I've spent my whole life in their society. I know how to blend in.

"Some of us are a little more powerful than others."

He doesn't miss the dig at his species, and I grin a little broader. He pauses for a moment, as if to collect himself.

"There are rules in Havenwood Falls."

"Which I'm sure you'll be more than happy to share with me." Resigned to my fate, I pull my jacket a little closer to my body. "Fine. Is there an adult who wants to talk to me?"

He doesn't like how I phrased that question, and I know it. But if he's going to talk down to me, I'm going to fight fire with fire. I could actually use some real fire at the moment, because Colorado is freaking cold.

"Sheriff Kasun wants to speak with you," the shifter finally says, as if coming to some conclusion. "Also, if you're planning on sticking around, you'll need to register and get your temporary tattoo."

"Why?"

"Think of it as a visitor's pass."

I roll my eyes but don't argue any further. No matter how much I may not like it, I need his help. And this town's. Once I figure out why that is, maybe I'll feel better.

"Fine. Then lead the way, Mr. Officer."

"It's Warren."

I pause, glancing up to meet his eyes. He puts out his hand, waiting for me to take it.

"I'm Warren."

After only a moment's hesitation, I take his offered hand.

"I'm Niccola."

When our skin touches, my whole body warms from the inside out. There's a moment when I think the space around us has lit up like a Christmas tree, and then I drop his hand, and I'm back in front of the high school once more. That is definitely not a response I've ever had to anybody. This town is just full of surprises.

# CHAPTER 3

*H*e leads me to a dark blue Toyota 4Runner, and I'm thankful the moment I'm inside and in the warmth of the car. Warren gets in without a word, turning the heater on right away.

"Is this a standard-issue police vehicle?" I ask, because I need to fix whatever this sudden weirdness is between us. What I felt when I touched him isn't normal for me, and it's making me off kilter.

"It's a trusty little thing."

The quick smile he flashes my way changes his whole demeanor. I wouldn't call him cuddly, but he's way more approachable. And if I thought he was gorgeous before, he's a bit breathtaking with that curve of his lips. Which are more than kissable, if I'm being honest.

Snatching my gaze away, I focus on the town outside the window. Shifters can pick up on a lot, so I need to be a little more controlled with my emotions. I don't need him sniffing out anything I don't want him to know. I'm also a bit shocked at myself. I don't remember the last time I was attracted to anyone like this. Actually, I'm going with never. My one barely-there boyfriend definitely doesn't count.

We pull up at the town square in no time at all. The police station is across the park from Coffee Haven. Maybe Willow alerted them to my presence, which just brings up another question as to why she would. But right now, I need to play nice and talk the sheriff into letting me stay, because like it or not, I feel like I need to stay.

Warren opens my door, taking me by surprise. At first, I'm taken by the gesture. No one has ever done that for me before, but then I realize he's probably just trying to get me out of the car. I've been sitting here for longer than I thought.

However, when we come to the police station door, he reaches in front of me to open that as well.

"Thanks," I mumble, not sure how to take the chivalrous move.

"You're welcome." And he sounds like he means it.

When we step inside, I'm not sure what I expect, but it's not the tan-colored walls. The place looks a little sad, but then, it is a police station. What immediately catches my eye are the two people standing in the front.

One is a man around my mother's age, taller than anyone I've ever met, with dark hair that is graying at the temples. He's dressed much like the rest of the town, in a flannel shirt and jeans. Even though he's not in uniform, I can tell he's the sheriff.

The other is a girl who appears to be a few years older than me, dressed in ripped jeans and a dark hoodie, with a pentagram on the front. She radiates confidence and authority, even with a nose ring. I like her instantly.

"Ric, this is Niccola." Warren makes the introductions, then steps to the side.

"Hi, sorry to cause such a stir in the cosmos." I try on a smile, but neither of the people in front of me relaxes. I think about putting out a hand, but I'm not sure if either of them would take it. Instead, I pull my jacket tighter, which has apparently become a nervous tic.

"I'm Sheriff Kasun," the man says, and surprisingly I find his voice soothing. "This is Adelaide."

"Addie," the girl speaks up, taking a step toward me. She does a quick scan with her eyes, and I wonder what she sees. I didn't even stop to look in a mirror when I stepped out of the airplane. After all the travel, I probably look the worse for wear.

"What brings you to Havenwood Falls, Niccola?" the girl asks, her full attention still on me.

"Honestly, I'm not sure." I decide to be up front about everything. "My mom—she's missing. All she left was this." I take out the note once more, as it has become my most precious commodity. Addie takes it, looking it over before passing it to the sheriff.

"I'm sorry that happened to you," Addie says, taking another step toward me. "What brought you here specifically?"

"I used a scrying spell for my mother, and that led me to Colorado. I'm not sure what possessed me to get into one of the vans, but I had no direction when I stepped off the airplane. This seemed like the right thing to do."

I pause briefly, then take a deep breath, deciding to put everything on the line. I glance at him, asking him with my eyes if I can talk to these people. I can tell they're supes, too. Addie's energy is similar to mine, so she must be a witch, as well as something else. Although witch is the dominant trait I'm picking up. The sheriff reads similar to Warren, so he's a shifter. But I need Warren's reassurance that I can trust them. He gives me a small nod, and I take that affirmation for what it is.

"Look, I'm not trying to cause any trouble. My mother and I are witches, and I can only imagine it was some kind of magic that led me here. I've had magic since I was five years old, and I know how to control it. I'll be eighteen in two months, and until then, I don't have any way of accessing my mother's records. Coven rules. I don't know my father. I don't know anything about this town. But if you would be willing to help me get some answers, I'll be out of your hair as fast as I can. Please. I don't . . . I don't have anyone else."

That last part is difficult to admit, but I know it's the right thing to say. It's that little bit of vulnerability that finally gets to them. I can see it in their faces. They exchange a look, then come to a decision.

"You may stay," the sheriff speaks up, before glancing over at Warren. "But you are to be accompanied by Warren at all times."

I open my mouth to protest, but Ric waves me off.

"This isn't open for discussion, I'm afraid. We'll have to discuss your stay with the Court of the Sun and the Moon, our governing body, so to speak. We have resources, and we can see if we can help. Warren knows this town. He'll be able to help you ask the right questions. Also, while you are here, please limit your magic use. We have strict rules about it."

I glance over at the shifter as he nods at the sheriff. In truth, I can't say that I'm surprised. I'd be suspicious too.

"Thank you," I say, turning my attention back to the sheriff. "I really appreciate it."

"We'll need to get you tattooed," Addie speaks up. "You look exhausted. I can do that in the morning. Do you have a place to stay?"

"Not yet."

"Warren can take you to the inn."

And that's that. Everything has been decided for me, and a part of me is glad. For the last two days, all I've done is keep myself afloat. I can't say that I trust these people completely, but I don't sense any wrongdoing from them. They're genuinely concerned for their town, and I can understand why I would make a few waves with my appearance. Especially since they know I have magic.

"Thank you," I say again, as Warren motions for me to follow him out.

The sun has set, and the temperature has dropped. I'm colder than I've been in my whole life, but I feel just a tad lighter. Because now I have a place to start and a plan. Somehow, I'm one step closer to finding my mom.

"We'll get you checked in at the inn. Where is the rest of your luggage?" Warren asks, as he opens the passenger door for me. Once again, I'm taken by surprise at his gesture, and it takes me a moment to reply.

"This is all I brought." I lift my shoulder, pointing to the backpack. He doesn't question it, just shuts the door and gets in at the driver's side.

"Hey," I begin, as he turns the warm air full blast, "I appreciate your help."

"Just doing my job," he replies, but it doesn't sound mean. That elusive smile graces his face for a moment, and I have to remind myself to breathe.

"You know, we could've just walked here," I say when we pull up to the inn.

"Yes, but you looked like you needed defrosting first."

He doesn't wait for my reply as he jumps out of the car. I get my own door this time, before he can get there.

"Don't fancy yourself a knight in shining armor." I raise my eyebrows at him. "You'd need a horse for that."

"Who says I don't have one?"

I can't help it. I chuckle. My outburst brings a full-blown smile to his face, and I stop in my tracks. My whole body warms up with that otherworldly fire once more, and it feels like we're the only two people in this town. It lasts only a moment, but I feel it everywhere.

"Come on," Warren says, and for some reason, I think he felt it too. There's a softness in those two words that wasn't there before. I don't reply, but follow him up to the inn. He opens the door for me, and I step into the warmth.

"Hey, Aurelia," Warren greets the girl behind the front desk. She's around my age and dressed like she's ready to walk down a catwalk at a fashion show.

"Hi, Warren. What brings you in?" She's all flirty smiles as she leans forward on one arm, her eyes on the deputy. She doesn't even spare me a glance, completely focused on the gorgeous guy beside me.

"Niccola here is visiting and needs a room, if you've got anything available." The girl swings her large brown eyes to me, giving me a once-over. I have no idea what she sees, but she's not impressed. She gives Warren another flirty smirk, then puts on her practiced customer smile for me.

"Sure, we have a room. Could you fill some information out for me, please?" She hands me a sheet of paper before turning back to Warren. She seems like she has to work at the whole being nice thing, but mostly her eyes are on Warren. I mean, whose wouldn't be? I fill out my information quickly as they chat, then hand it over.

"There's a dining room here, but if you'd like, I can come pick you up at eight, and we can grab breakfast before we meet up with Addie," Warren says, as Aurelia types my information into the computer. She's not very chatty with me. A few more clicks and she's handing me a key.

"Your room is upstairs. Enjoy your stay." That customer smile is back in place, though she glances over at Warren. He doesn't seem to notice, still waiting for my answer.

"Yes, that would work," I reply quickly, but I don't move. I'm not sure why I'm feeling so awkward, but here we are.

"Let's see that room." Warren takes the key from my hands and heads toward the stairs. A second later, my brain kicks into action, and I hurry after him. Okay, I really need to reel in my teenage hormones. I'm becoming a complete mess.

Warren doesn't seem to have any reservations, though. He marches right to my room, unlocking it and letting me go in first. I step inside and study my surroundings quickly. The bed looks the most inviting, and I can't wait to lie down.

"You've got one of the private bathroom rooms," Warren comments, stopping in front of the second door.

"I didn't know that was an option."

Warren chuckles, taking a few steps toward me.

"Get some rest, Niccola. You'll be safe here." He places the key into my hand, his fingers lingering on my skin for a second longer than necessary. I glance up, once again fascinated by the dark blue of his eyes.

"Nic."

"What?"

"My friends call me Nic."

He smiles, disarming me completely. Then he steps back, walking over to the door and swinging it open.

"Good night, Nic." And just like that, he's gone.

# CHAPTER 4

*T*take a long, hot shower, washing away the last two days. My hair has become a tangled mess, and there are smudges of mascara under my eyes. What a great first impression I've made on this town.

When I'm in my pajamas, I climb into the bed, reaching for my phone. There are no messages, no phone calls. The coven won't wonder where I am until sometime tomorrow. Then someone will probably reach out. But Mom and I keep to ourselves most of the time. I'm not exactly popular with our people.

I have a secret.

The only thing my father has ever given me is a shifter gene.

That's right. I'm half witch, half shifter. Not winning any popularity contests with that one. I'll have to tell the sheriff this, and maybe that tattoo chick. But I don't want to tell Warren.

Witches and shifters aren't exactly known to play nice. And we are definitely not supposed to break out of our own circles to fall in love. My mind instantly drifts to Warren and the undeniable pull I feel toward him. Is it my shifter side calling to him? Or something else?

I lie back down, wondering if I'll sleep at all, and when I close my eyes, the tears I've been holding at bay for days spill out. Clutching a pillow to my chest, I let it all out.

The pain.

The fear.

The loneliness.

For just this moment, I'm a kid once again. I want my mom, and that is as simply as I can put it.

It's with tears in my eyes that I finally fall asleep.

When I wake up next, I'm surprised to see that it's morning. I expected nightmares to keep me awake once again, but I slept right through. Stretching my hands over my head, I consider just staying in bed all day and forgetting about the horror that's become my life. I'm all on my own, with no one to turn to.

I grab my phone, seeing that I have about forty minutes before Warren arrives. Maybe I'm not so alone after all. There's something about him that keeps me intrigued in a way I'm not used to. Also, he's hot, and I'm not blind.

After a quick shower, I pull on my trusty T-shirt and jeans combo, then braid my hair down my back. Because I'm still a teenage girl who's about to hang out with a very hot guy, I swipe some eyeliner and mascara onto my eyes. They're bleaker than I'm used to, but that's what happens when your whole life falls apart. When I reach for my red lipstick, there's a knock on the door. With a few quick swipes, I have my battle armor on, so I head to the door.

Pulling it open, I'm greeted by a spine-tingling sight. Once again in jeans, this time Warren is sporting a dark blue pullover sweater that makes his eyes look even deeper. A coat is draped over one arm, and his other hand is in his pocket. He stares at me as if he's never seen me before.

"Good morning?" I make it a question because I'm completely unsure of myself for the first time in a very long time. But the way he's looking at me is making all of my insides melt, and I don't know how to handle that.

"Good morning." He finally seems to come back to himself. "Here." He thrusts his coat at me, as if it's on fire.

"What?"

"You'll need it."

"I have a jacket." I wave my hand in the direction of my room, where my very thin jacket is visible on the bed.

"That won't be enough."

A part of me wants to continue arguing, since I don't really have people controlling me on the regular. But I quickly realize that's not what he's doing. He's concerned, and after last night, I can see why. I was basically a popsicle when I got to my room.

"Thanks," I mumble, unused to this kind of chivalry. He's got a lot of that in his blood. I pull the material over my shoulders, instantly swallowed up inside the warmth. Warren watches me a moment longer, then clears his throat.

"Shall we?"

I nod and step back inside long enough to grab my room key, phone, and credit card. Warren leads the way down the stairs, and the moment we're outside, I am beyond thankful for the coat. This weather is not something I'm used to. I might've thought that a time or two already.

"What kind of breakfast would you like?"

"Quick one. And one that involves a big cup of coffee," I reply instantly. Warren chuckles, and I'm warmer than I was a second ago.

"Coffee Haven it is."

When we walk into the cafe, I feel that calming presence washing over me once more. This time, however, I'm not sure if it's the place or the company. Warren greets the same woman I ordered from yesterday before turning to me.

"We weren't properly introduced yesterday," she says, giving me a small smile. "I'm Willow."

"Nic," I reply, looking from her to Warren. "Were you . . ."

"The one to call the sheriff? Yes. I won't apologize for that."

"I don't expect you to."

That earns me another smile, before Warren orders his coffee and I order mine, with a scone once again. There's no one in front of us, so we get our breakfast and take a seat at one of the tables. I want to say something, anything, but I have no idea where to start.

"I know I said this yesterday," Warren beats me to it, then pauses to take a sip of coffee. "But I'm sorry about your mom. It must be tough."

I shrug, which is my typical response for any conversation about emotion, but Warren doesn't buy it. He watches me carefully, but there's no pity in his gaze. Just quiet understanding. Maybe that's what prompts me to say what I do next.

"It's just me and her. My whole life. I feel a bit lost without her."

"That's understandable," he says, and I think he means it. "But I won't let you wander away."

His words make the world disappear for one split second so that all I see is him. The pull I've felt toward him since the moment we met wraps around me like a heavy blanket, then he's the one to break the eye contact.

"Where would you like to start today?" he asks, clearing his throat.

"Besides going to meet the tattoo chick?" I ask with a smile. He returns it, with a quick nod. "I was thinking of maybe trying another locator spell? Now that I'm in Colorado, maybe I can try reaching out toward my mom's energy."

"I don't know if it'll work within the town's limits. You're protected while you're here, and no one can find you," Warren says carefully, and I nod.

"Of course, duh. Maybe you can drive me to the outskirts?"

It's the best I got, but it makes sense. And Warren seems to agree. When I'm finished with my scone, we take our coffee to go, and he leads the way toward the police station. There's no one inside, which seems strange, but it's not like I know anything about small-town business. I turn to Warren, but before I can ask a question, the doors open, and Addie walks in.

"Let's do this," she says by way of greeting. I look at Warren, and he motions for me to follow Addie.

"Okay, girl. The tattoo can be visible or invisible. It'll disappear either way when you leave town. I spoke to the Court, and they're letting you stay until you find what you need about your mother. But listen carefully. If you display any kind of magic, or break any rules, you're out. Number one rule: don't harm the humans. Number two: protect our secret."

"Understood," I reply immediately, and that seems to pacify her. I don't think any of these people will trust me any time soon, but I will do whatever it takes to let them know I will play by their rules. I have no other choice.

"I can sketch out whatever you'd like," Addie continues. "Visible or invisible?"

I don't even have to think about it.

"Visible." I lift my left arm, pointing to a spot below my thumb on my wrist. "Right here."

"A girl who knows what she wants." Addie smiles, her pencil ready to go.

"A jasmine flower, on a branch."

"We're heading outside the wards for a locator spell," he tells Addie, and she nods before getting to work.

It takes her less than a minute to sketch the perfect delicate tattoo and about twice that long to have it on my wrist. When she stands, she gives me one long look before turning to Warren.

"I added a bit of extra magic. The tattoo and her memory will keep. But don't stay long." They exchange a look I don't understand, then she leaves.

My eyes are drawn back to the tattoo now residing on my wrist, and I wish it wasn't temporary. It's small and beautiful, and it reminds me of the first time I felt in control of my magic.

"What does it mean?" Warren's soft voice breaks through my thoughts. At first, I don't want to tell him. But when I meet his eyes, it's like I don't have a choice anymore.

"I was eight when I finally found my center," I almost whisper, unable to look away from him. "My magic had been out of control for two years, and I made a mess of things in the park. I had to hide in a jasmine bush, and when my mother finally found me, I found my control."

I glance down at the flower on my wrist, overwhelmed with emotion. I push it all back, shutting it away for later examination, then tug the jacket over my shoulders again, covering up the memories.

"Shall we?" I ask, echoing his earlier words. He grins and leads the way.

~

When we make our way to his truck, the town is fully awake. Without using my magic, I can't discern whether the people passing us on the street are supernaturals or not, but either way, I'm amazed at this community.

I'm also fascinated with the boy walking beside me. There are so many questions running around in my mind. He's a shifter, but how old is he really? And what kind of a shifter is he? And does he feel the weird pull between us or is this just my response to him?

That last one is the question that's bugging me the most, because I am not the type of girl who swoons over guys, but that is the only thing I want to do when I'm around Warren. This is definitely not the time or place, but here we are.

"You might as well ask." Warren's words break through my thoughts, snapping me back to reality. At first, I'm terrified he can read my thoughts, but then he continues. "I can see that you have a lot of questions about this place. Most people do. You can ask, and I'll try to answer."

"Because I won't remember any of this anyway?"

Not sure why, but that question makes me ridiculously sad for a second, and I have to school my features into a neutral expression before I give it away. I'm also not the kind of girl who's open with her emotions, but it's all I can do to keep it all bottled up right now. Which is understandable, considering my mother is missing, but it's not constructive, so I need to reel that in. And fast.

"The memory wards are necessary," Warren says, and it sounds like even he's a little sad about that fact. We study each other in silence for a moment, before I'm the one to look away.

"Tell me about yourself," I ask, if only to keep him talking. I like the sound of his voice.

"Well, you guessed it right. I am . . . what you said I was." I smile at that as a few people push past us. "The sheriff and his mate found me when I was barely even a pup and adopted me for the first few years. Then there was some unrest within the pack about letting me stay, and I was sent away to live with another . . . family."

My heart squeezes at his words, and I can see why he understands my search so well. He knows what it feels like to be alone. Suddenly, the desire to reach out and hold his hand almost overpowers me, so instead, I stuff my hands into his jacket and stay silent as he talks.

"Jefferson took me in and raised me as one of his own. Hawthorne is a town run by the Hawthorne coven, and their community lives and works closely with shifters. When it was time for me to leave, I ended up here. Angry and lost, because . . ."

He pauses for moment, as if trying to find the words, and I can see the pain in his eyes as clear as day. This time, I don't hesitate. I reach for his hand, taking it in my own. His gaze narrows on the spot our skin touches, and I swear my whole body is on fire.

"Gabriele, Ric's love, she died giving birth to the twins. She was the only mother I knew, and I didn't even remember her. Not until it all came crashing back."

"Do you wish the memory wards kept you from remembering?"

I'm not sure what prompts me to ask such a personal question. Maybe it's the way Warren's thumb keeps making circles on my skin. Maybe it's his proximity. But when he meets my eyes, it's like he's been waiting for this exact question.

"Yes and no. I'm glad I have those memories of her back. But they brought a lot of pain with them. Something I've had to deal with."

"I can understand that," I say, because it's how I feel about my father. "I think I would like to know who my dad was, but also wouldn't. It's a strange place to be."

"It is."

And just like that, I think we've reached a point in our new acquaintance where we're no longer strangers. He understands the cracked parts of me, because he's got plenty of his own. Even though it's an unsteady foundation, it feels surer than anything in my seventeen years of life.

When Warren starts walking again, he doesn't let go of my hand, and I hold on just as tightly.

# CHAPTER 5

*W*hen we drive past the town's limits, a part of me grows sad. One day soon, I'll be doing that for real, without a chance to ever come back. I'm not sure how a place can get under my skin in less than two days, but I feel it.

"We should move fast," Warren says, as we get out of the car some time later. I nod, understanding the urgency. Without much hesitation, I plop myself on a fallen tree, reaching for my phone and crystal.

"Do you need anything else?" Warren asks, and I understand the confusion. Most witches scry with much more than a phone and a crystal. But my intuitive magic helps amp up my spell without anything extra.

"I'm good," I say, before I place the phone on the log beside me and close my eyes. The crystal warms up once more, this time more intensely than before. Instead of keeping it inside my palm, I uncurl my fingers from around it.

"Nic!" Warren's voice snaps my attention to him, and I open my eyes to glance at him. But he's watching me. I look over and find the crystal hovering over my hand.

"What?" I ask, but then quickly push the questions aside. The crystal is still buzzing with the spell, so I focus my intention on it, keeping my focus strong. What happens next takes me completely by surprise, and it's a moment before I'm on my feet. The crystal zooms away, as if being pulled in a particular direction.

"Come on!" Warren reaches for me, and I barely have time to grab my phone. Hand in hand, we take off after the crystal. After almost ten minutes, we're barely keeping up with it. Suddenly, with a whoosh, it imbeds itself into a tree, making the forest around it echo from the impact.

Warren and I stop, then approach it carefully. There seems to be a small opening in the trunk, but I'm not sure if I should reach for it.

"Has that ever happened to you before?" Warren asks, and I shake my head.

"Can't say that it has," I reply, still not taking my eyes off the tree. "But I was doing a locator spell for my mom. I doubt she's in the tree." And I'm not picking anything up from the area. It's like my magic has gone completely dormant.

"Let me try something," Warren says, and then I feel the air around me move. Glancing over, I come face to face with a gorgeous dark colored wolf. My mouth drops open, and I quickly close it. There are no articles of clothes, so he must be charmed to keep them within his shift. I've heard of it before, but have never seen it myself. The magic fascinates me, and maybe I'll be brave enough to ask him about it one day.

I swear Warren grins at me before he walks over to the tree. I know shifters have heightened senses, even more so in their animal form. So when he begins to sniff the area, I don't interrupt. After a few moments, he turns back to me, as if giving me the go-ahead.

Carefully, I make my way to the tree and reach for my crystal. I work at the opening, prying it apart, until a piece of paper falls out. I feel Warren move toward me, and realize he's shifted back. For some reason, I can't bring myself to reach for the paper, so he stoops down and grabs it.

"It's a diploma," he says, bringing my attention to him.

"What?"

"From Havenwood Falls High. It's made out to Matilda Nile."

I jerk at the name, stepping closer to look at it myself. Warren sees the change in me, the rigid way I hold myself, sensing my mood before I can even pinpoint what I'm feeling.

"What is it?"

"That's my grandmother," I whisper.

~

We hike back over to the truck in silence. Warren is giving me the time I need to process what we've found, but I can't wrap my mind around it.

"My grandmother died when I was three years old" was all I said before he led me away from the tree. I've only ever known her from my mother's stories. She was a powerful reader witch, which is where my mother gets her powers from. But she died suddenly, as far as I know, and that's when Mom settled us in California.

"I don't understand this, Warren," I speak up, as we cross back into the town's limits. He glances over at me, then looks back to the road.

"Mom must've lived here, when she was a teenager," I continue. "But she never mentioned it. She never told me where my grandmother was from, just that she was gone."

"Nic, she couldn't have, remember?" Warren says, keeping his voice soft. "The town's memory wards would've wiped your grandmother's and mother's memories when they left."

"But she left a clue anyway."

"Are you sure it was your grandma who did that?"

"What do you mean?" I ask, as Warren pulls up in front of the inn and parks.

"It could've been your mother, which is why the spell found it when you were searching for her. Maybe she was here too."

I mull that over, staring out the windshield, as a few tourists walk by. The more answers I find, the more questions pour in. Was I actually led to this town by accident, or did something call me here? I don't understand any of this, and I just want my mom.

"Hey." Warren is the one to reach out this time, taking my hand into his. "We'll figure this out. This is a good place to find answers. And you've got pretty great help."

I chuckle as he grins at me, surprisingly feeling better. It seems that I don't know much of anything anymore, but I do know that I'm not alone. Somehow, I was led to this town and to Warren. Of that, I have no doubt. Whatever comes next, I can handle it.

Taking a calming breath, I look up at Warren and give him a small smile.

"I think we should go to the school."

# CHAPTER 6

*T*he school looks just as intimidating as it did yesterday. Warren leads me inside, and the empty halls instantly get to me. I've never gone to an actual high school. Even though I'm supposed to be graduating this year, I'm at least a semester behind. It would be so interesting to go to this school, to be part of the regular hustle and bustle of a teenage lifestyle. Something I don't have much of.

"Do you have any idea what we're looking for?" Warren asks, stopping right inside the front doors.

"No," I reply honestly, and try not to feel frustrated by that fact. After all, that's why we're here. To see if we can figure this out. "Maybe we can walk around and see if anything jumps out at me?"

"Sounds good."

We fall into silence as we begin wandering the halls. Some of the lights are on, and I briefly wonder if a teacher is here working on some lesson plans. I think teaching would be an interesting career and something I've thought about pursuing more than once. But since I can't even graduate from high school, I'm not sure how well received that'll be.

We stop in the main hallway, in front of the trophy display case. I look over the awards and the silver-and-blue paraphernalia everywhere.

The case goes from floor to ceiling, with dark wooden trim and four shelves in each section. Two jerseys hang against the wall; they look like football and basketball to me. There are quite a few medals and certificates, as well as a few large trophies.

"The mascot is a dragon? Of course," I comment.

Warren chuckles beside me and turns to go when my eyes zero in on a photograph. I glance down at the plaque that reads *Basketball – Conference Champions, 1990*. Next to it is a picture of the team and a few other guys. It looks like they were on some camping retreat. My eyes roam over each person, unsure of what exactly made me pause when I saw it. Warren must notice the way my body tenses, because he's back at my side.

"What is it?"

"I'm not sure," I reply, then pull out my phone. Opening the photo app, I scroll through, my heart beating so hard I think it's going to jump out of my chest. Warren moves closer, as if offering his support, because I'm sure he can sense my anxiety even without his supernatural hearing.

When I stop scrolling, my eyes don't believe what they see. It's almost like I've lost all ability to breathe, and I force myself to inhale.

"Nic?"

"It's . . . him," I whisper, looking up and studying the picture in the display once more.

"Who?"

"My father."

Warren turns immediately, eyes zeroed in on the photo, before I show him the phone. The picture I have is taken maybe ten years later, the one piece of him that my mother kept in her album. When I was little, I used to open it up to see if I was going to look like him. When I got this phone, I took a picture of the photo, just in case.

"He went here?" I mumble, my mind racing. How is this possible? What does it mean?

Warren takes my hand, pulling me around to face him.

"Hey, breathe, okay?"

I don't even realize I'm shaking until Warren is pulling me into his arms. I cling to him as if my life depends on it, as the emotions bombard me on every side. After all this time, every notion I had about my father is closer to realization than ever before. This is where he went to high school. Maybe even grew up. This makes him more real than he's ever been to me, and I don't know what to do with that information. So I do the only thing I can and hold Warren close, hoping that I can hold myself together a little longer.

I sit across from Warren at Burger Bar, staring at the cup of water in front of me as if it holds the answers to the universe. Honestly, I don't even remember walking across the street or into the restaurant.

"Do you want something to eat?" Warren asks, breaking my concentration. I glance up at him, finding concern there, and my heart squeezes at the sight. We're way past acquaintances now, and I'm a bit embarrassed at how clingy I was with him.

"Maybe just some soda?"

He nods and goes to order, giving me a moment to myself. I have so many questions, but no idea what to do next. For years, I thought mom made him up, telling me romantic stories of a witch and a shifter who fell in love. It was very Romeo and Juliet, until it came to the same tragic end. Now I have definite proof of not only his existence, but of his history. And of my grandmother's, apparently. I've only ever known of my grandmother outside of this place, but what if my mother was here too? There are just too many variables. When Warren sits down in front of me, he pushes a cup of soda my way with a smile.

"The fizzy water always helps me too." He shrugs, and he looks younger than before, with that boyish grin on his lips. My heart flips, but for completely different reasons this time, and I take a sip just to do something. I'm probably blushing like crazy.

"You really had no idea?" he asks as I swallow, and my eyes fly back to his. I shake my head.

"I didn't even think he was real half the time. But now I find out he lived here? In the same town as my grandmother. That's crazy to me. I don't even know what to do!'

"I have an idea."

I put the next fry down, leaning over the table. "I'm all ears."

Warren chuckles at my enthusiasm, then leans back and stretches.

"Seriously?" I roll my eyes, and this time he laughs outright. I let the sound wash over me and instantly feel better. I know what he's doing, and I appreciate it oh so much.

"I think," he says, leaning toward me across the table, "that we should talk to some of the people in that photograph."

"Wait, I didn't even think of that!"

"I mean, I am training to be a full-fledged police officer." He leans back, spreading his arms out in front of him. "I'm pretty good at this."

I grin, and my heart feels lighter already. In this moment, I am so thankful Warren is here to help, because I'm so caught up in my emotions, I couldn't even see the next plausible step.

"Okay, so we should get the names and start there?"

Warren pulls out his phone, putting it on the table between us. I didn't even see him take the picture, but there it is. Grainy but recognizable. He points to the person to the right of my father.

"You've already met this person."

I stare at it for a second and then sit back in my chair. "The sheriff?"

"The sheriff," Warren agrees, taking his phone back. "We should talk to Rusty as well. He's been around long enough that he would've met your father."

"Paul."

"What?"

"His name is Paul. That's all I really know about him. I don't even know his last name. I've always just been Niccola Steven." The sadness is so heavy on my chest, I wonder if I look down, I'll see it as a physical weight. I feel a whisper of a touch on my hand and glance over just in time to see Warren place his hand over my own on the table.

"We'll figure it out, Nic," he says, looking deeply into my eyes. "You are not alone in this."

We watch each other quietly, the noise of Burger Bar fading into the background. Warren and I started on such a rocky ground, and now I can't imagine doing this without him. I never understood how my mom could've been so madly in love at such a young age. But now, here I am going through the exact same experience I've always found so doubtful.

I pull my hand back, giving him a small smile. But I can't let myself feel anything for him. I mean, once I have my answers, I'll be leaving. And forgetting all about him and this place. I realize I don't want to forget him, and that's a dangerous place to be.

I need to be more careful about my thoughts and my emotions in this town. Who knows if there's someone here who reads thoughts? And I know shifters can pick up on more than what's visible to the human eye. I'm already plenty embarrassed. I don't need to make a bigger fool of myself.

When we get up to go, the question I've been sitting on bursts out of me.

"How old are you?"

Warren stops for a moment, then his eyes flash, and he smiles. "I'm twenty-one."

"Actual twenty-one?"

"Yes." He chuckles. "Actual twenty-one."

I nod, but don't comment further. This is all the confirmation I need. Guys like him don't fall for teenagers like me. He's just a genuinely kind shifter, and I can't allow myself to mistake his concern for something it's not. I'm becoming the cliché I hate. I'm the girl with the unrequited infatuation with an older guy. Just what I needed.

# CHAPTER 7

"The sheriff will meet us at the library," Warren says as we walk out of Burger Bar. The temperature has dropped another few degrees, and I wonder where my shifter gene is because I am cold. Unlike Warren, who barely has a sweater on.

"Why the library?" I ask, as I burrow deeper into Warren's jacket. I don't think I'm ever giving it back at this point. I catch the quick smile he throws my way and think I'm never getting my heart back either. Is that a fair trade? His jacket for my heart?

"It'll be easier to talk in there. It's pretty quiet at this time of the day and year."

I don't argue, and in no time at all, we're standing in front of a beautiful gothic Victorian-style house straight out of some novel. There is a definite charm to this town. And it has nothing to do with the guy standing beside me.

When we walk inside, I am greeted by a vast foyer and the smell of books. Since I've always wanted to be a teacher, books are kind of my best companions. This place is more beautiful than I can put into words.

Sheriff Kasun is already there, with another man who looks to be in his late twenties. He's dressed much like the sheriff, in flannel and jeans, and I briefly wonder if this is just a pack uniform at this point. I almost chuckle at my stupid thoughts, but decide against it. I need to work on making better first impressions.

"Hello, Niccola. Warren." The sheriff greets us as we walk up to the two of them. The other man turns, his brown eyes serious and calculating. I can't imagine him smiling easily, but man, do they make them sexy in this town. He looks like he could be featured in a magazine article entitled "Sexy Mountain Men."

And now I'm fidgeting under Warren's jacket, because I'm pretty sure they can smell my hormones at this point. What is wrong with me?

"This is Rusty. He may be able to help you."

I nod, not trusting my voice as I follow the men up the stairs and to the second floor, which I find out is called the Ravenal Wing. My fingers itch to pick up and study each of the beautiful books I see on the shelves, but I resist. Maybe after it's all said and done, I can come back here and explore. Shaking my head, I try to focus. Warren looks at me, waiting for me to speak up.

"We found a picture at the school," I begin, and Warren pulls his phone out to show the others. "The man next to you is my father."

Ric glances up and meets my eyes. I can't read him, but I let him study me for a few tense minutes. But then it's Rusty who speaks up.

"I can see it in your eyes." We all turn to look at him, as he takes a step closer. "I remember him. He was only here for four years. He left a year after graduating."

"Do you know his last name? Or where he might've gone?" The excitement and anxiety rise up as one, and I try to keep myself from bombarding Rusty with more questions.

"He didn't tell anyone he was leaving. One day, he was just gone. Left his family and girlfriend behind. You look a little like her too."

"My mom? You knew my mom?" So she was here; it wasn't just my grandmother. For some reason, I thought they met outside of this place, but now I see I can't assume anything.

"Lissa. Yes. She was a sweet girl. For a witch."

His words take me aback, but then I realize he's making a joke. His eyes sparkle for just a moment, and I relax, as Warren and Ric chuckle. I like this man.

"All I have is this picture of him," I say, pulling up the photo on my phone. The men in front of me study it, then share a look.

"That wasn't taken anywhere here," Rusty comments. "Not that I know of, at least. It could've been sometime after he left. Lissa left a year after him and never came back. As far as I know, Steve hasn't crossed the boundary since the day he left."

I freeze, whatever question I had dying on my lips. Warren moves toward me, a comforting presence at my back.

"What did you just say?" I whisper, my blood running cold. "What did you call him?"

"Steve. Steven. That was his name."

"And his last name?" Warren asks, realizing at the same moment what I'm trying to get at. Ric and Rusty exchange another look before Rusty answers.

"Knight. Steven Knight."

"Do you . . ." I'm almost afraid to ask. "Do you know my mother's last name?"

"Summers. Lissa Summers."

My world shifts for what seems like the tenth time in so many days. I step away from the men, my head spinning. My vision tunnels, and my magic races to the surface, as I struggle to breathe. I can hear voices all around me, but they sound so far away. Nothing is how it's supposed to be. I can't get air into my lungs.

Suddenly, there are arms around me, pulling me around, and then Warren's face comes into focus.

"Breathe, Nic. Breathe."

His voice pushes through the panic, and as I focus on him, I come back to myself. We're on the floor, and he's holding me on his lap, cradling me as if he can protect me from everything in this world. I bury my face into his shoulder, trying to pull myself together.

"I don't know what happened," I mumble.

"You had a panic attack," Warren says, and I can feel his reply against my cheek. I've never felt safer than I do in this moment, and that realization makes me push against him. I can't let myself become this person, but it's already too late.

"Can you explain your reaction?" the sheriff asks, as I pull away from Warren and stand. I forgot they were here for a second. After I straighten my clothes, I turn to the two men.

"Apparently, my mother has lied to me my whole life." I shrug, trying not to let the panic back in. "She told me my name was Niccola Steven. I carried my dad's name with me this whole time, and I didn't even know it. I don't know anything. I don't have anybody. No one I can trust."

Tears stream down my face as suddenly as the panic attack hit. I can't meet anyone's eyes, so I push past them and run down the stairs and out the door. I don't know where I'm going. I just know I need to get away. I wish I could run from my problems as easily as I ran out of the library. But that's not how things work.

All I feel is betrayed and scared, and I no longer just want my mom. I want the truth.

~

I end up at the town square once again. My whole body feels numb, and it's not just the cold. I keep expecting someone to come after me, but they don't. Maybe they understand I need a minute to process.

A sign on a building catches my eye: *Havenwood Falls Music and More.* The "and" is a musical clef symbol, and it makes me smile. I push the doors open, walking into the store. It smells clean and fresh, and it's calming somehow. I've stopped crying, but I'm on the verge of starting again.

I've never been a musically inclined person, but I've always loved music. As I study the instruments hanging on the wall, I wonder if my dad knows how to play any. The thought instantly brings tears to my eyes.

"Hello there," a quiet voice sounds from behind me, and I turn to see a petite blonde offering me a comforting smile. She studies me, and it feels as if she can see right into me. The silver cross around her neck sparkles as she almost glides toward me, and for some reason, I lose it all over again. I'm crying before I know it.

"Oh, sweetheart," she says, stepping closer to me and placing a comforting hand on my upper arm. "Can I help?"

"I don't think anyone can help," I hiccup, embarrassed at my display of emotion.

"I can listen."

And apparently, that's all the invitation I need before I'm telling her everything. Minus the magic parts. As I talk to her, I can feel the anxiety leaving my body. She doesn't interrupt or ask questions. Just lets me get it all out.

"I'm sorry," I finally say, wiping at my eyes. "I don't know what came over me."

"You miss your mom, even though you feel like she betrayed you. It's perfectly normal. No matter what she's done, she's still your mother. I'm Cece, by the way."

"Thank you, Cece. I'm Nic," I say, because even talking it all out made me feel so much better. She seems like she carries all the wisdom in the world, and I want to ask her opinion on so many things. Warren included.

The doors open, bringing cold air with them, and at first, I think it's going to be him. But it's a woman, and my eyes are instantly drawn to her dark hair and red highlights. I've wanted to do that to my hair for ages, but Mom always says no.

"Are you ready to go?" The question dies on her lips as she sees me.

"Sherry, this is Nic. She's going through a rough time right now. What do you say we take her to lunch with us?"

"Oh, no. I wouldn't want to intrude." If my mother has done something right, it's that she raised me with manners. The two women exchange a look like they're on the same wavelength.

"Nonsense, Nic," Sherry says, giving me a comforting smile. "We would love to take you with us."

Looking from one woman to the other, I feel like this is exactly what I need.

"If you really think it's okay," I say, with a tentative smile. Sherry doesn't hesitate to return it, sliding her arm through the crook of my own and leading me toward the door. Cece is right behind us, and in no time at all, we're back at Coffee Haven.

Cece and I find a table, while Sherry goes to order. Even being in their presence is lifting my spirits already. They're not my mother, but they're the older, wiser guidance I need right now. I've never felt more like a kid than I do today.

"It's my treat," Sherry says, placing a cup of coffee and a scone in front of me. "It's blueberry and my favorite." She doesn't wait for a response, just turns and walks back to grab her coffee and Cece's.

"Thank you," I say when Sherry takes a seat. "I . . . thank you for being nice to me." I think I might start crying again, and I don't understand where all this emotion is coming from. It's taking all I have not to make a scene.

"You can talk to us, Nic," Sherry says, reaching over and placing her hand on my arm. I glance up, because even though I just spilled a lot of my worries on Cece, I'm still not done. Without hesitation, I give Sherry the same rundown I gave Cece. Both of the women listen carefully and fully, making me feel like I'm the most important person in their lives at this moment.

"People have a tendency to disappoint us," Sherry says, her voice soft and comforting. "Even our parents are not immune to that. I'm not trying to excuse what your mother did, but maybe she had a good reason."

"But it's not like I can ask her!" I snap, instantly ashamed at my outburst. "I'm sorry, I just . . . I don't have anyone but her. What if I don't find her? I'm seventeen. I need my mom. I need a home. I don't even have that anymore."

What I said is true. I don't think that apartment will ever feel like home again. I feel more so here, in this town, than I ever did in Palmdale.

I wonder if the two women in front of me are supernatural. With my emotions such a mess, unless I call on my magic, I can't quite discern it, but I don't want to push my luck and get kicked out for my curiosity. Warren will probably know. The moment I think of him, my body heats up.

"Home isn't always a place, Nic," Cece says, her voice that same comforting tone it was in her store. "Don't lose hope that you will be able to find that again."

And I'm thinking about Warren again. Maybe this isn't the best place and time, but I need to talk to someone about him. Even after this small acquaintance, I feel like I can trust these women. Which is very unusual for me.

"Do you believe in fate?" I blurt, before I chicken out. I glance up at Cece, and there's a quiet sadness in her eyes that makes me pause. She smiles, but even with my untrained eye, I know there's a story there.

"I do," Sherry replies, bringing my attention back to her. There's a dreamy look about her, and it makes me curious.

"So you think people are meant to be together?"

"Absolutely. Some people just connect, like two pieces of a puzzle. It's almost like magic."

The word makes me pause, but I don't question it. Because I understand. It's how I feel when I'm around Warren. It's like we're in our own world, and I feel safe with him.

"Do you . . . do you think you have to be a certain age to experience something like that?"

Sherry and Cece exchange a look, then Cece asks, "Is there someone specific you have in mind?"

My first instinct is to deny it, but then I realize I'll never get the answers I'm searching for if I keep hiding from my own feelings. So I lower my voice, leaning towards them, before I reply.

"There's a guy . . ."

"I knew it," Cece whispers, moving forward as if she doesn't want to miss a single word.

"Cece loves a good love story." Sherry chuckles, glancing at her friend. "And so do I."

"I wouldn't call it a love story," I reply, instantly embarrassed. "Maybe I shouldn't have said anything."

"You don't have to share anything you don't want to, but if it helps?"

I grin at Sherry and Cece and their eagerness. Maybe they need this as much as I do. Throwing caution to the wind, I decide I have nothing to lose and everything to gain.

"I just never met anyone like him before." I begin, keeping my voice low. I don't need any supernaturals overhearing my confession. "I've had one boyfriend, last year, if you could really call him that. But I always thought destiny was just something grownups used as a way to justify their decisions. I mean, if destiny was real, wouldn't my parents still be together?"

"Sometimes people love each other deeply, but their paths separate at some point, never to intersect again," Cece says, and a part of me thinks she's speaking from experience. "It doesn't mean that their destiny wasn't to fall in love. It just means that that point in their lives made them who they needed to be."

I mull over those words, understanding them in a way I wouldn't have two weeks ago. My mom has always loved me, and done what is best for me. She must've loved my dad very much to give him up, if that's what happened.

"You don't think seventeen is too young to find that kind of a connection?" I'm almost terrified of the answer, but I have to know.

"I think only you could really know the answer to that," Sherry replies. "But in my personal opinion, love doesn't have an age to it."

I think that over, and I feel the seed of hope within me soaking it up. Yet, I still can't let it become a full-blown plant. There are so many obstacles in front of me. The biggest one being that this is all one-sided.

"What if it's just you, feeling it, I mean."

"As in unrequited?" Cece asks, as I take a sip of my coffee. It's grown lukewarm since I've been sitting here, spilling my guts to two strangers. If only Mom could see me now. She'd be as surprised as I feel.

"Yeah. I'm not exactly his type. Or his age."

And there it is, boiled down to the simplest terms. He's clearly out of high school; I can't even graduate. I don't even know how many credits I would need at this point. Plus, I'm a complete stranger, passing through town. My love for books has made me a romantic.

"Age is a tricky business, but we can't really give you more unless we know more," Sherry says carefully. I know she doesn't want to intrude, but I'm sure she knows Warren, and it would be weird if I said something.

Right?

Maybe.

I'm so confused.

Before I can make a decision, the doors open and in walks the guy of the moment. His eyes instantly find mine, and I can see the relief in them at seeing me. The sheriff and Rusty are right behind him.

"Hey, you!" Sherry exclaims, jumping to her feet and launching herself at Rusty. They share a kiss that makes me even more wishful than I already am. "What brings you here?"

"We've been looking for Nic," he says, glancing over at me, and I feel guilty for making them worry. The others greet Cece as well, but Warren hasn't taken his eyes off me.

"Are you okay?" he asks, stopping on the other side of the table. I nod, not trusting my own voice, and that's when I feel Sherry's and Cece's eyes on me. They glance from me to Warren, settling back on me. Without a doubt in my mind, I know they know it's him I've been talking about. I duck my head, unable to meet their eyes. Why did I open my big mouth in the first place?

"If you're up to it, we can go see if we can find more information at the library?" Warren continues, but I suddenly come to a decision.

"Actually, I was hoping to go back to the inn. I think . . . I think I need to lie down."

"That's a great idea," Sherry comments, smiling down at me.

"Okay, I'll walk you there," Warren says, but Sherry is already shaking her head.

"We'll take her," she says as Cece stands up as well. Warren glances between the two women, a bit confused, then turns to me. I don't think I can handle being in his presence right now, so I stand as well, moving to Cece's side.

"I'll see you later, okay?" I say, moving past him to the door. With a quick goodbye to the sheriff and Rusty, I leave them behind. It doesn't take long for Cece and Sherry to catch up to me.

"So, that's him?" Cece asks, keeping her voice gentle, and all I can do is nod.

"Four years isn't that much of an age gap. Not in our world."

I glance at her sharply, wondering what exactly she means by that. Because she can't really mean that she knows. Can it? I think Sherry might, considering she's in a relationship with a shifter, but I don't feel any magic in her. Not without sensing further.

"Don't look so scared." Sherry chuckles. "We know all about Havenwood Falls."

"I'm not sure what you mean," I say, trying to keep myself from giving up too much.

"You don't think I know Rusty is a shifter?" Sherry asks, grinning at me.

"And you are?"

"Human."

"But it works?"

I think of my own heritage—a witch and a shifter. It's been taboo for so long, I've never met anyone who was comfortable with such a drastic difference in species.

"He's the love of my life," Sherry replies, and I believe her.

"What about you? Are you human too?"

"Far from it. I'm an angel," Cece replies. At first, I don't think I hear her right. But she's completely serious, and that literally stops me in my tracks. Cece and Sherry pivot to face me, waiting for me to digest that information.

"Wow, I mean, wow. I've never met one before. That's . . ."

"Wow?" Cece smiles, and now I can see why her presence is so comforting to me. She's actually a being of light. Instantly, I feel embarrassed by my petty problems.

"Hey," she says, taking a step toward me. "I am here to help, no matter what problems arise."

"Can you read my mind?"

"No, but I can read you. You carry a lot of weight on your shoulders for someone so young. It's not an easy position to be in, but you are strong. Even stronger than you give yourself credit for. Of that, I have no doubt."

Tears pool in my eyes, and then I do another very uncharacteristic thing for me. I take a step toward her, and Cece opens up her arms as I fall into them. She hugs me close, and I can feel her comforting touch even through the layers of my clothes and Warren's jacket. It's a brief hug, but one I needed very much.

"I'm sorry about that," I hiccup, wiping at my face.

"You needed it more than you needed words." Cece smiles, patting my arm. And just like that, I feel better.

"Would you like me to bring you some clothes?" Sherry asks, when we arrive at the inn. "Or a jacket?"

I glance down at myself, pulling Warren's coat closer to me. It's true that I'm not really great at accepting help, but this is something else. I don't want to give up this piece of Warren that I have.

"I'm okay, but thank you."

"Don't hesitate to come by if you need anything," Cece says, Sherry nodding in agreement. I watch the two women, amazed by their differences and their friendship. They belong in this town. I wonder what it would feel like to belong.

"Thank you so much for your help today. I know I came out of nowhere and—"

"You are welcome," Sherry interrupts before I start apologizing. She hugs me quickly and tightly to her body, then steps back. "We're here for you, Nic. You are not alone."

"Warren told me the same thing," I find myself saying.

"You should listen to him," Cece comments, smiling warmly.

"And you should let him in a little," Sherry adds, pulling my collar a little tighter. "I think you both can use it."

They don't stick around any longer, waving as they head back toward Cece's store. I get myself inside the inn and up the stairs without meeting anyone's eye. A big part of me was running from Warren back there, but the moment I'm inside the room, I realize just how tired I really am. Without shedding the jacket, I lie on top of the covers and close my eyes. For the first time in days, I fall asleep instantly, with fresh tears still on my cheeks.

# CHAPTER 8

*A* knocking pulls me out of my dreamless sleep, and I sit up, rubbing my eyes gently. The knock comes again, and I realize someone is at my door. The light outside the window is gone, and I wonder how long I've been asleep. Padding over to the door, I swing it open to find Warren on the other side.

"Hi." He looks a little unsure of his welcome, which is understandable. I've been acting very irrationally where he's concerned. "Did I wake you?"

"What time is it?" I run my hand over my hair, wondering if I look as unbalanced as I feel.

"A little after seven. I thought you'd be hungry."

I slept for a few hours, but I guess my body needed it. The moment Warren mentions food, my stomach growls. He chuckles, and I roll my eyes. Of course this would happen to me.

"I guess that answers that." He smiles, catching me by surprise. Just like every other time. There's just something about him when his lips curl up that sends my world spinning. "Would you like to go to dinner with me?"

I stare at him for way too long, finally nodding my head. Motioning for him to come inside, I shed his jacket and hurry into the bathroom. Checking myself in the mirror, I see that my eyeliner is all gone, leaving some black streaks on my eyelids. But at least my mascara is mostly in place, since it's waterproof. My hair is a squished mess, having been in a braid all day and then slept on.

As quickly as I can, I fix my makeup, donning my trusty red lipstick, then take another look at my hair. Pulling the elastic out, I unbraid it and run my fingers through it, letting it fall around me in loose waves. Re-braiding it will take too long, so I leave it down and step into the room.

"I'm ready."

Warren has been staring out the window, but he turns at the sound of my voice. He freezes at the sight of me, as if seeing me for the first time. I want to say something, anything, but I've lost all control of my motor functions. A lock of hair falls forward over my shoulder, and it's like that small movement spurs him into action.

"Here, I brought you this," he says, coming to stand in front of me as he pulls something out of his back pocket. "It's colder out now since it's dark. I thought you could use it."

I look down and find him holding what looks like a dark beanie. Glancing up, I go back to staring instead of taking the offered gift. Warren watches me for a moment longer, then closes the rest of the distance between us and pulls the beanie over my head. His fingers graze my face, sending a shiver up my spine. We're standing way too close, and as I look up at him, I realize I would stay here forever.

"Thank you," I say, barely above whisper.

"You're welcome," he replies, his breath warm on my cheek. It wouldn't take much for me to reach over and pull him down to my level. To wrap my arms around his neck and find out if his lips feel as soft as they look. But no matter how brave I may be, in this moment, I'm terrified.

Of these feelings.

Of myself.

"We should get going," Warren says, taking a step back with a small smile. I'm not sure if it was him or me who moved away first, but he must've seen it in my eyes. I reach for his coat, and when I pull it over my shoulders, I turn and find him watching me. He smiles quickly before he gestures toward the door.

The moment we're outside the inn, I'm thankful for the hat. The wind has picked up a bit, and I burrow myself deeper into the jacket. Warren stays close beside me, and my hand itches to reach for his. I really need to get a hold of my stupid hormones.

"What sounds good?" Warren asks, pulling me back to the here and now.

"Pizza," I answer immediately, and he chuckles.

"Perfect. Because Napoli's is just across the square."

We begin our walk, taking our time. It's like neither one of us is in a hurry. I look for something to say, but the silence isn't uncomfortable, which is also new for me.

"Are you doing okay? With all of this, I mean?" Warren asks after a moment.

"You mean the part where everything I've ever known about my family or myself is a lie? And I'm homeless and motherless? Sure, I'm doing great. So great."

My sarcasm isn't wasted as Warren laughs, and the sound warms me even more than the coat does.

"It's a lot. I can't even imagine," he says. "But you're handling it better than I could."

"Oh, I don't know about that."

"I do."

His tone is serious, and I sneak a peek at him. He looks like he really believes what he's saying, and that makes me feel better.

"Hey, Warren!"

A girl's voice sounds before I can say anything else, and we turn as one to see a beautiful blonde heading our way. She's holding hands with a guy, who's a little less blond, but just as cute. They look to be about my age, but I really should stop guessing ages. In this place, nothing is sure.

"Hey, Celeste. Jonathan."

The boy nods his head in greeting, but doesn't speak up. He looks like a bad boy in his black leather jacket, while she looks fashionable enough that I would like to be friends with her.

"Where are you headed to?" the girl, Celeste, asks, as her eyes swing briefly to me.

"Napoli's. Celeste, this is Nic. Nic, this is Celeste and her boyfriend Jonathan. I volunteer at their high school from time to time."

"It's nice to meet you both," I say, offering a smile, which is easily returned by the two. Of course Warren volunteers. I've noticed firsthand his kindheartedness.

"We're headed to Napoli's too!" Celeste says, beaming. "Can we join you?"

Warren and I exchange a look. Even though a big part of me wants him all to myself, I know that's it's probably better if we have company.

"Of course," I'm the one to reply, and we turn as one toward the restaurant. It's not far, and once inside, Celeste and I find a booth, while Jonathan and Warren go to say hi to a group of guys at a table.

"So what brings you to Havenwood Falls?" she asks, not beating around the bush.

"I'm actually looking for my mom. And dad," I add as an afterthought, thinking I probably should've come up with a cover story. But it's too late now. A lot of people already know why I'm here. If these two aren't aware of the supernatural aspect, it's a bit of an unbelievable story, but it's what I have to work with, so there's no turning back now. I pull the hat off my head, patting my hair down.

"What happened to your parents?"

"Well, I've never met my dad. I just know he's from here. Mom sent me this way to see if I can find him, I guess?" That seems legit enough.

Celeste studies me with a puzzled expression on her face.

"I know, it sounds crazy to me too." I shrug.

"So you don't know your dad at all?" she asks, as the boys return, taking a seat. Warren's body slides into the booth beside mine, and I can feel the heat off him instantly. It takes some serious self-control not to lean into him.

"No. I mean, I know what he looks like. And I now know that he went to Havenwood Falls High."

"That's where we go!" Celeste exclaims, leaning a little against Jonathan. He really doesn't seem like the talkative type, but he seems nice at the same time. Go figure.

"I'm a senior this year. I'm pretty excited. We both are. Are you in school?"

Just then a waitress comes over, and we order some drinks and a pepperoni pizza.

"I'm supposed to be," I reply honestly, as soon as she's gone. "But I've never been to an actual high school."

I can feel Warren's eyes on me as I talk, but I don't want to look at him. If I look at him, I'm afraid I'll spill all my insecurities in front of him.

"How is that possible? How old are you?"

"I'm almost eighteen. But I've mostly been homeschooled. And taught in a small classroom setting by our . . . friend," I almost say coven leader. I need to be more careful.

"Jonathan was homeschooled too!" Celeste says, turning to her boyfriend.

"I was," he agrees, speaking up for the first time. It's fascinating to see their dynamic. Celeste doesn't seem like someone who is used to being in the background. It's like she expects people to listen to her. But Jonathan is completely content being almost invisible.

"How do you like Havenwood Falls High, then? Is it really different?" I find myself asking, because apparently I want to torture myself with the knowledge. Up until coming to this town, I didn't realize how badly I was missing out on the whole high school experience.

"It's not bad. I'm pretty new to it myself, but it's got some perks," he replies, giving his girlfriend a look that makes me smile. They're adorable. It's the best word I can find for them. Our pizza arrives then, and we dig in as if we haven't eaten in days. That's definitely what I feel like, even though it's only been a few hours.

"Is that all you know about your dad?" Celeste asks, once I've polished off a piece of pizza.

"Well, today we found out that he played basketball. He was on the team that won a championship in the nineties."

"Wait." Celeste sits up taller, her full attention on me. "What year did he graduate?"

"1990, we think?"

"Oh my goodness, my dad played basketball in high school!"

"Seriously?"

I turn to Warren. "Let her see the picture."

He pulls out his phone, and I make a mental note to get the picture from him, when Celeste looks up at me.

"That's my dad!" She points to a man two over on the left of my father.

"That's mine," I say, pointing to him. "Do you think your dad remembers him?"

"I would think so. My dad has a pretty good memory. He's an accountant, so he kind of has to."

"That's amazing," I breathe out, my heart once again anxious and excited at the same time.

"You can totally come over and talk to him. We can go tonight," Celeste announces, taking a bite of pizza. I meet her eyes as she grins at me, and I answer in kind.

"Thank you so much," I say, turning to Warren. He looks just as excited as I feel. That need to reach out fills me once more, but he beats me to it. His hand covers my own on my lap, squeezing it briefly, and that small touch makes my heart soar.

We finish up our food fast, because I can barely sit still from excitement. Talking to the sheriff and Rusty has provided us with some information, and I'm nervous to see what else this town can tell me about my family.

It doesn't take us long to get to Celeste's house, and she's shouting for her dad the moment we're inside. Warren takes my jacket and hat, placing it by the door in the foyer. Before we take two steps, a man in his late forties rounds the corner. He looks approachable, which makes me feel better instantly.

"What's all the shouting about?"

"Hi, Dad. Meet Nic. She's got some questions for you about her dad," Celeste says, before she takes Jonathan's hand and drags him behind her and into what I'm assuming is the living room.

"Hello, Nic," Celeste's dad says. "I'm Brian. How can I help you?" He nods at Warren in greeting, but his attention is completely on me.

"I'm not sure if you remember him," I begin, a little shaky. Warren's hand wraps around mine tightly, and I hold on with all my might as I turn the phone toward Brian. "The man two to your right. He's my father. I don't know much about him. Just his name . . ."

"Steven," Brian says softly, studying the photograph before looking up at me. "You look like him."

His words bring tears to my eyes, but I hold them back. Now is definitely not the time. Brian motions for us to follow him. We end up in the living room, where Celeste and Jonathan are already on the couch. Warren and I take a seat, not breaking contact, and I'm thankful he's here. Brian walks over to a shelf, pulling out a book. He walks back over as he leafs through it, then hands it to me.

It's a photo album. There in the middle of a plastic sleeve is my dad, his arm around Brian, both of them holding basketballs over their heads. They're grinning, and my heart squeezes at the sight of him.

"He was one of the best players on our team," Brian says, a faraway look in his eyes. "We were close. Our whole team was pretty close. I sometimes felt like he was holding back, though, when we played. He was funny too. Always kept us laughing."

Brian takes off his glasses, running his hands over his face before replacing them. I wonder if my dad would have a bit of gray in his hair, or if his shifter gene keeps that from happening. I can't even begin to guess how old he really is.

"Do you know what happened to him?" I ask.

"No. One day he was just gone. Lissa was heartbroken. He didn't tell her he was leaving. They'd made a lot of plans for the future. They had this journal, where they would write everything down. Lissa carried it with her religiously."

"My mom," I say, and Brian meets my eyes once more.

"You're Lissa's girl? So she found him."

"Found him?"

"She swore she would, after he left. It took her almost a year, but then she left too and never returned. Her mother left a few years after. I always hoped they found each other. Seeing you, that means they did."

"I guess," I say, not sure how to respond to that. "He didn't stick around."

"That doesn't sound like him."

"What do you mean?"

"He was fearlessly loyal. And he loved your mom more than anything. If he left, there had to be a life or death situation in play. I didn't think anything could keep those two apart. It's like they were destined to be together."

I glance at Warren, and he's already looking at me. Maybe he feels it too, that intense reaction to the whole destiny thing. Because when he's near, I absolutely believe in fate.

"I'm sorry I don't have more information for you," Brian says, and I shake my head.

"No, you gave me a glimpse into who he was. That's not something I had before." Which is true. Rusty and Ric mentioned my mom, but this was different. Brian and my father must've been close.

"Thank you," I say to Brian, then glance over at Celeste. "Thank you for bringing me here."

"Of course," she replies with a smile.

When Warren and I leave, I don't know what to say or do. I definitely don't know what to feel. But I know that every single person

I've met in this town has somehow given me a gift. They've given me clues to help find not only my parents, but myself. Warren included.

I look over at him now as he waits me out, letting me come to terms with what we found out. After all that, I have one huge question that I want to ask him, but I don't know if I should. The fact that I keep second guessing my every move is frustrating and very unlike me. But I guess that's what happens when you're no longer standing on solid ground. I can't seem to find my footing.

Annoyed with myself and my lack of courage, I stop walking. Warren turns, inclining his head at my sudden stop.

"Do you believe in fate?"

This seems to be the question I need the answer to most lately. Maybe it's because of my parents. Maybe it's because of him. But I need to know what he thinks about it. It's become an actual need deep inside me.

He doesn't answer right away, and I'm afraid I've shown too much with my question. After what seems like an eternity, he walks back over to me, standing close enough that I can feel his body heat.

"I do," he finally answers, and I let that wash over me. I don't know what I'm expecting or what I'm looking for.

"You think people are meant to find each other? That there's some cosmic balance that's fulfilled when they do?" My chest feels heavy, and I think I'm on the verge of another panic attack. I've never had one, not until that moment in the library, when I found out my mother lied to me. But now, I feel the pressure for a whole lot of different reasons. Mainly because I know when I leave, all of this will cease to exist for me. And I don't know how I will ever survive that kind of loss. I think I'll feel it even if I don't remember it.

"I think some people are destined to cross paths, in a way that changes their lives forever. Ric and Gaby were my first evidence of that. They found me, they saved me, and I think that was meant to be. Sending me to live with Jefferson wouldn't have happened if it wasn't for the Kasuns."

Of course he thinks I'm talking about family. I shake my head, glancing down at my feet. His priorities are where mine should be, but I'm over here swooning because of a pretty face.

"Thanks for your help today," I say, changing the subject abruptly. He watches me curiously, but doesn't comment, waiting me out. He does that a lot. It's like he understands that I need to stay in some sort of control over my life. If only in this one aspect.

"We can start early tomorrow."

I glance up at that, meeting his eyes. "You're going to keep helping?"

"Of course." He flashes that smile I'm becoming ridiculously attached to. "We'll figure this out, Nic. I know it."

"Thanks, Mr. Officer."

"You're welcome."

# CHAPTER 9

The next morning, I'm up even earlier. Warren and I spend the whole day in the library, looking up old records, but find nearly nothing new. There are yearbooks from the years my dad was in school here, but outside of a few pictures, there's not much information. I do find a picture of my mom and dad together, her smiling up at him, as he looks at the camera. They're inside the gym— I can see the bleachers in the background—and they look happier than I've ever seen.

Warren and I keep up a steady conversation throughout the day, and the more he talks, the more I like him. When I go to sleep that night, I dream of him and wake up sadder than I should be. I'm not sure what I dreamt, only that it led to heartbreak. So basically, kind of like my life right now.

The next two days go by in the same manner. Nothing new, just more time spent with Warren and the inevitable truth that I will eventually be leaving, just like my parents did. And never returning. It's the fourth day that finally brings some results.

"Look at this," I say, pulling up a photograph I found at the back of a yearbook. This one is a year after my parents graduated, so I didn't look at it until now. But there is my mom, standing beside my dad, in

Town Square Park. She's holding a book tightly against her stomach, as he leans over her shoulder toward the camera.

"I've seen this book before."

I grab my phone and pull up the picture I took of the yearbook photo earlier. There they are, in the gym, the same book pressed against her side.

"Do you remember Brian mentioning a book they shared? With all their plans?" Warren asks, looking up at me.

"Yes. This must be it, right? I mean, these photos were taken a year apart, and she still has it."

"You've never seen it before?"

"No. I guess it would be too much to hope that she kept it, but I've never seen it. It must've been too painful, you know. To keep it."

"But she wouldn't have remembered," Warren reminds me gently, and there they are, those frustrating memory wards.

"There has to be a way that she did. How else would she have met up with my father outside this place?"

"Maybe they didn't remember each other, but their love still guided them to the same place, at the same time."

I glance up sharply, my gaze colliding with Warren's. He sounds almost wishful, and the intensity in his eyes makes my head spin. He doesn't take his eyes off me as he speaks.

"Maybe they felt so strongly about one another that no matter what magic came between them, they were still led to each other."

"Do you think that's possible?" I whisper, afraid of the answer and looking for it all the same.

"I do. I think love is the strongest magic there is."

"Have you ever been in love?" I'm surprised by my own words, but I don't regret them. I need to know. Because what I feel for him, it's more than I ever thought possible. It doesn't matter that I'm only seventeen. I can't deny myself these emotions.

"No, never before."

And I don't know why that makes me feel lightheaded. Why it turns my world upside down once more. He's not telling me he loves me. It's too soon for both of us. But . . . I still hope; I still yearn for that to be true. And so I'm the first to break eye contact. It's the way things have to be.

I stare at the picture of my parents, and I want to ask them so many questions. One of which is whether I can trust what I'm feeling for Warren. My whole life I was taught that teenagers don't know the meaning of true love, but this thing between us, it's bigger than anything I've ever imagined. Regardless of how he feels, it has shaped me forever.

"Do you have any idea where such a book might be kept?" I finally ask, focusing on the task at hand. Warren is silent for a moment, so I'm forced to face him. He's watching me steadily, and only when our eyes meet does he reply.

"I don't."

"Would the library have it in storage?"

"Not this library, unfortunately. There was a fire. This place only opened up a few years ago."

I almost groan out loud, but it really isn't Warren's, or the library's, fault. Getting up, I begin to pace, walking from shelf to shelf.

"The only thing I can come up with," Warren says, bringing my attention back to him, "is going back to the school. Maybe we missed something."

I nod, because it sounds like our best move. But not tonight. Tonight, I just want to rest and not think about anything.

"We can do that in the morning, right?" I ask, and receive one of Warren's smiles. He's begun to understand my moods, almost better than I do myself. Standing up, he reaches for his jacket, holding it out for me. I step into its warmth, pulling it close around me. I wonder if I can take it with me when the time comes to leave.

Just like that, I'm back here again, in this sad and lonely place. I want to find my mother. I want to know more about my dad. But I also want to stay in Havenwood Falls. And that's a new one for me.

Warren parks at the inn, then comes around the front and opens the door for me. He's been trying to keep me as warm as possible. I give him a small thanks, and we begin to walk toward the front doors when we're stopped.

"Warren!" a guy's voice calls from behind us, and we turn to see a cute blond boy and a pretty petite girl heading our way. There's something in the way they're holding hands that makes me take notice. It's like they're afraid one of them will disappear.

"Joe! You're back."

The two hug in that manly, pat on the back kind of way, beaming at each other. The girl stays quiet, grinning at the two of them, until Warren turns to her.

"If it isn't Infiniti." He gives the girl a quick hug as she says hello.

"Nichols," the blond guy says, "you finally talked them into giving you a badge."

Warren laughs, turning my attention back to him. He's comfortable with these two, in a way I haven't seen before. There's a deep-rooted friendship here, mostly with the guy, and it raises plenty of questions. I guess I'll just add them to my always growing list.

"They let you guys out of prison for the holidays?"

"It's college, not prison." Joe chuckles, pulling Infiniti closer to him once more. It's like he has to keep his hands on her at all times, and from what I can see, she's soaking it up. My heart thuds in awareness, but I push the jealousy aside. It's only wishful thinking on my part, and I keep my eyes on the couple instead of Warren, just to prove to myself that I can.

"This is Nic," Warren says, bringing me into the conversation. Both Joe and Infiniti turn to me as one, assessing me quickly. Infiniti seems like a free spirit, but she's cautious. Joe is territorial, and I wonder if he's from Warren's pack. That would explain their familiarity.

"Welcome to Havenwood Falls," Joe says, and I focus back on him.

"How do you know I'm new around here?"

"I've been here my whole life." He smiles at me, and I feel better. He's not trying to pry, but when you live in a small town, visitors must stand out.

"How do you like it?" Joe asks, and I shrug a little in response.

"It has its perks, I guess."

That makes the group laugh, and for a moment, I feel like I belong here. With them. In this town.

"Fin is pretty new to it herself, but she tells me she wouldn't want to be anywhere else," Joe says, and the pretty girl snuggles closer. They look so in love, it's blinding.

They share a look that's only meant for the two of them, and this time I can't help it; I glance over at Warren. His eyes are already on me, and it's like the intensity Joe and Infiniti have is being passed on to the two of us. I need someone to teach me how to not make a fool out of myself anytime I'm around Warren. It's becoming a problem.

Warren and Joe seem like they have something to discuss, so I step to the side, turning to face Town Square Park. A moment later, Joe steps up beside me, and I glance over to see Infiniti on the phone and Warren talking to an elderly gentleman.

"Whatever brought you here, Warren is a good guy to have on your side."

I glance at him sharply, wondering how much he knows.

"He's helping me find my mom. And dad, I guess."

"It sounds like there's a story there."

"There is. It's one I've been telling a lot lately." The sadness comes fast, like an arrow slicing through my shoulder. Even though a part of me is still mad, at this moment, I miss my mom something fierce.

"We all have stories." Joe breaks through my thoughts, and I look over to find him watching Infiniti. "This place is good for that. I think you are all led here for a purpose. It'll be interesting to see yours, Nic."

Joe can't be a year or two older than me, but there's depth in his eyes of someone who has been through a trial or two. Infiniti comes up then, and they reach for each other at the same time. Whatever they may have gone through, it brought them together, and that's something that gives me hope.

"It was nice to meet you, Nic," Joe says, then with a small wave, he and Infiniti walk off. Warren comes up to stand beside me, but doesn't say anything at first.

"What was that all about?" I finally ask, shifting from foot to foot. It's getting colder by the minute.

"Joe was just giving me some friendly advice," Warren replies, turning to head back to the inn. I don't pry further than that, even though I want to. We walk in silence until Warren speaks up. "He told me not to get myself in trouble."

"What does that mean?"

"It means he knows from firsthand experience what it feels like when someone leaves this town and the memory wards kick in. He knows what it's like to live with losing someone."

"You mean Infiniti?"

"They've had quite an ordeal, that's for sure." Warren's expression turns serious for a moment, and my curiosity is piqued. We reach the inn, and he follows me inside. The warmth makes me feel better instantly, and when I turn to say goodbye, he shakes his head. "I'll see you to your room."

I don't argue, for once, because after today, we both need this time together. Soon, I'll be leaving. And when I do, I'll be forgetting everything about this place. I want to scream in frustration, at the top of my lungs, because what I found here is something I've never had. Home. Friends. A place where I belong. A place where I don't have to hide.

"Warren, there's something I have to tell you," I say, unlocking my door. He stops just on the other side of the doorway, and after a moment, I motion him inside. Shedding his jacket, I go to the window, too restless to sit.

"Maybe I should've told you this earlier, but it's something I haven't shared with many. It may change the way you look at me. Maybe. I'm not sure. I'm afraid it might."

Without turning around, I know he's moved to stand behind me. I can feel his heat reaching out toward me, as if coaxing me to speak up. Still not looking at him, I push the words past my lips.

"I'm not just a witch, Warren. I'm half shifter. My dad was a shifter. That's the only thing I truly know about him."

I say it all in one breath, my body shaking at the thought of what this could mean. Warren might walk out of this room and never return. But I know I had to tell him. It was no longer a secret I could keep.

He doesn't say anything, and I'm too afraid to turn around. But then I feel his hands on my arms as he gently turns me to face him.

"I guess we do have something in common after all," he says softly, and the tears I've been fighting spill over onto my cheeks. I laugh and cry at the same time, as I work at getting a hold of myself.

"You're not . . . disgusted?" I finally manage through all the emotion.

"This just makes you more of who you are."

I launch myself at him, all reservations forgotten, and he catches me easily in his arms. We stand like that, body to body, and he holds me just as tightly as I cling to him. With all of my heart and soul, I beg the universe that I never forget this moment or how it feels, for as long as I live.

# CHAPTER 10

*T*'m sleeping worse every night. The impending doom of me leaving brings with it nightmares. My constant worry for my mom doesn't help either. We have to find out something before I run out of time.

My dreams are keeping me restless. I know I'm dreaming, but I can't seem to pull myself out of the nightmare. There's my mom, bloodied and bruised, lying in the middle of Town Square Park.

*"Why did you let this happen?" she whispers, looking up at me as I reach down to help. The accusing tone makes me pause, and then there are more of them.*

*Warren. My dad. Ric. Sherry. They're all around me, all bleeding and watching me like it's all my fault.*

*"I didn't mean for this to happen," I shout, trying to convince them, as well as myself. But I stand accused, and when they begin to close in on me, all I can do is scream.*

I sit up in my bed with a jerk, sweat dripping down my back. The light pours in through the half-closed curtain, drawing my attention to it as I orient myself. My phone buzzes, and it's a text from Warren saying he'll be a few minutes late. Pushing all thoughts of the dream out of my mind, I jump out of bed and get ready.

When Warren shows up at my door, there are two cups of coffee in his hands. And a blueberry scone in his pocket.

"You're a lifesaver." I thank him, accepting the cup eagerly. A part of me thinks that I will need a refill a few times today. I'm bundled up in Warren's coat and hat, with jeans and boots on, and I'm still chilly when we step outside.

"Let's take the truck." Warren motions me forward, and I could hug him. It takes us much less time to get to the school this way. I'm lost in my own thoughts, and Warren doesn't try to make small talk, for which I am very thankful. Just being in his company is comforting, and I need all the comfort I can get right now.

The school is still on break, so there's almost no one there. Especially this early. We wander the halls, visiting some of the classrooms. Once again, I wonder how it would feel to go to a school such as this. I can feel the history of this place, but also the way it fits in the here and now. That's a special kind of teenage magic I've never known.

When we step inside the gym, my breath catches. Slowly, deliberately, I walk toward the place my parents stood all those years ago when that picture was taken. My head spins with memories and emotions, and I can't tell which are mine and which are just remnants in this place.

"They must've been in love, right?" I find myself asking out loud. Warren walks up to stand in front of me, watching me carefully.

"I believe they were."

"Then something horrible must've happened to keep them apart."

"Sometimes . . ." I thought he would agree with me, but there's something else here. I glance at him sharply, catching his eye. "Sometimes, it's not a life or death situation. Sometimes it's just a decision that's best for both parties."

The way he watches me . . . for the first time, I think he feels it too. The invisible pull we have toward each other, despite the age difference and the present circumstances. He gets me, in ways I don't fully understand myself. My heart doesn't want to hope, and it doesn't want to let go of what's standing so close within reach.

We move as one, as if being tugged together. Warren reaches for my hand, holding it tightly in his, as I place my other hand over his heart. I can't look away, even if I tried. The intensity of his gaze roots me to the spot, and when he leans down, I know this is the moment I will remember for the rest of my life.

But when I close my eyes, I'm somewhere else. The magic—actual magic—pulls me in, and without a second thought, I answer in kind. The bright light behind my eyelids becomes unbearable, and I squeeze them tighter. Images and voices begin to assault me on every side. I scream, stumbling, but I can't get away. Or get out.

Warren's voice sounds somewhere far away, but I'm still lost in the brightness. Magic washes over me, and then a door opens with an audible click. I pinpoint the sound, pulling myself toward it, and then I'm hurtling through.

Then everything goes black.

~

Voices sound all around me, and I try to sort them out. Warren's is the first one I understand.

"Is there anything you can do to wake her?" he asks, his voice laced with concern. I want to open my eyes and tell him I'm awake, but I can't seem to muster up enough energy. Panic sets in, making it hard to breathe. Or was it already hard to breathe? I can't tell. It feels like I'm spinning out of control.

I feel my body dip to the right, as if someone has sat down next to me, and then Warren's voice is much closer.

"It's okay, Niccola," he whispers, before I feel his touch on my forehead. "I'm here. Everything will be okay." His voice soothes me, and after a few feeble attempts to open my eyes, I decide to save my strength and listen.

"Whatever has her under, it's not our magic," a vaguely familiar voice speaks. "From what I can tell, it's as if she stepped through a spell specifically attuned to her."

"Like blood magic?"

"Yes." The room grows quiet for a moment before the voice speaks up again. "She has to pull herself out of it. All we can do is make her comfortable."

There's a commotion, and I think more people are in the room, if that's where I am. It feels like I'm lying on a bed, so we must've migrated from the gym. Which is the last thing I remember.

The brightness.

The rush of power.

And then nothing.

Before I can do anything else, I'm fading.

The next time I wake up, the room is dark. I manage to open my eyes, just barely, and I find that I'm back in my room at the inn. A chair has been pulled up to the bed, and a very tired Warren is sitting in it, lost in thought.

I must move before I can think too much about it, because Warren's eyes snap over to mine and he's instantly moving toward me.

"Nic, hey," he whispers, as I turn my face to the side. I feel clammy all over, my body alternating between hot and cold.

"What happened?" I barely manage, trying to force more air into my lungs.

"You're sick," he replies, reaching for something on the table before bringing it in front of my face. It's a glass of water and a straw. He lifts me, just a bit, and I drink my fill. After I'm finished, he sets it back on the table, then props me up further. For a second I think I'm going to fade again, but somehow I hold on.

"How long have I been out?"

"Two days."

"What?" I glance at him sharply, making my head spin with the jerky movement.

"Hey, take it easy. You've been in and out. Addie tried to see if they can break through the spell, but nothing worked. I was . . . terrified."

Warren's voice is but a whisper at that last word, and it squeezes at my heart. I've come to see him as this strong capable figure, but here he is, a bit vulnerable at my bedside.

"I'm okay," I say, reaching out and placing my hand over his where it rests on the bed. His eyes zero in on the contact, and I can see his shoulders relax. It's as if he's been waiting for this specific moment.

"There's one more thing," he says, looking up at me once more.

"What is it?"

"Your hair . . ."

I reach for my locks immediately, but they're still there. Confusion shadows my vision, but then Warren reaches over and brings a lock in front of my face. I look down to find my hair no longer brown, but silver.

"What happened?" I want to jump up and go look at myself in the mirror, because if there is one thing I love about myself, it is my hair. When I turned eighteen I was going to experiment with different colors and styles, as a rite of passage, since it's always grown so fast anyway.

"It started changing when you passed out. We don't know what it means. Or if it'll last."

"I need to see," I say softly, holding tears at bay. I never thought of myself as a vain girl, but my hair was something that was mine. Suddenly, Warren's arms are around me, and he's lifting me up.

"What are you doing?" I would've squealed if I had that much energy. He holds me close to his body, and I entwine my hand around his neck.

"Helping you see."

He carries me over to the bathroom, placing me carefully on the countertop. We're almost eye to eye, and at first, he's all I can look at. My stomach is filled with nervous butterflies as I watch his own eyes darken in awareness. I lick my lips, and his gaze flickers there before it's back on mine. I think this is the moment I've dreamed about my whole life, as he leans closer. But before our lips can touch, the door to my room opens, and Ric walks in, followed by Cece.

"How are you feeling?" the angel asks, giving me a quick study.

"Awake," I reply, glancing in the mirror. My hair is completely silver, matted and dirty from sweat, but still very shiny.

"Glad to see you up." Cece directs my attention back to her. "We were worried." She glances at Warren, then gives me a warm smile. I'm sure I'm blushing.

"I don't know what happened," I say, shrugging my shoulders. "Something clicked in that gym. I remember my head spinning and being blinded by a light and then everything going dark."

"Nothing else?"

"No, I . . ." My mouth stops working as my head spins once more. Warren catches me in his arms before I can topple off the counter, cradling me to his chest. I cling to him as if my life depends on it, pushing the dizziness away.

"Get her back to bed," I hear Ric say, before I'm being carried once again. Warren places me gently on top of the covers, and before I can form a coherent thought, I'm gone.

∼

The next time I'm fully awake, I'm so thirsty I can't even swallow. I know I've been in and out, but at this moment, I'm finally feeling a bit like me. Raising myself onto my elbows, I look around and find Warren sleeping. He's still in the chair, but his head is on the bed next to my legs. He looks so young with his eyes closed. I think it's because I can't see the intensity behind them, the history he carries with him. The desire to run my fingers through his hair is uncontrollable. It's soft to the touch, as delicate as a feather.

He opens his eyes, but doesn't move, and for some reason, I don't stop. I continue my exploration, growing bolder to the point where I move my fingers lightly over his cheek and chin. His lids fall for a second, then he's looking at me once more. There's that intensity I've come to admire. I pull my hand back as he sits up.

"You look better," he says, studying me as if his life depends on it.

"I feel less . . ." I try to say, but my throat is dry. Warren reaches over and hands me a cup of water, and I drain it completely. "I feel less . . . unbalanced," I reply honestly, not sure what I mean by that but knowing it's true.

"You've been out for a while."

"How long is a while?"

"Three days."

I gasp, shocked at losing so much time. Five days in total that I've been completely out of commission. It feels like I've been hit with a very bad flu. My whole body feels sticky, and I'm pretty sure I smell.

"Tell me what happened."

"You had a fever for two straight days. Then your body temperature went the opposite direction, moving to cold then hot again, and we couldn't elicit any kind of responses. There was magic at work, unlike anything this place has seen."

I don't remember anything, so it's not like I can give him any answers. Instead, I ask him another question.

"Did you stay with me the whole time?" I whisper.

"I did," he replies, not breaking eye contact. I'm not sure what this thing inside me is, but right here and now it grows into something huge. And I know without a shadow of a doubt that Warren is it for me. Maybe it's crazy to know that at a young age, but I don't think I will ever meet another person, human or supernatural, who's going to fit into the crook of my heart like Warren does.

"Can you stay a while longer?" I ask.

"I'm not going anywhere."

And it feels like a promise that goes much further than staying with me today.

"I'd like to take a shower," I say, scooting down the bed. Warren doesn't hesitate. He stands, pulling me carefully with him and leading me to the bathroom.

"I'll be here."

I take that promise and tuck it into my heart. Forever.

# CHAPTER 11

$\mathcal{T}$he water feels heavenly against my skin. I wash my now silver hair, still amazed at the change. I'll have to figure out if there is a reason for this, just like there must've been for the spell. I focus on trying to remember anything from when I was out. There's something nagging at the back of my mind that I can't quite pinpoint. There were colors and numbers and emotions, but nothing I can hold on to for long. A knocking on the door makes me jump.

"Are you okay?" Warren's voice comes through muffled.

"Almost done," I reply. As quickly as I can, I dry off and put on my pajamas. Carefully, with calculated moves, I make it out of the bathroom in one piece. Warren is standing by the window and turns when I walk out.

"I called Ric, letting him know you're much better. He's relieved. He'll let the others know."

I nod, but don't comment, making my way slowly to the bed. I'm sure I'll be interrogated a few times, but I have nothing new to tell them. This is the time when I would ask my mom for help.

"Hey." Warren is suddenly kneeling in front of me, his eyes full of concern. "It's going to be okay."

He reaches over, catching a stray tear, and that's when I realize I'm crying. Everything in my life feels so unmanageable. I've been spinning out of control since I found our apartment in disarray. The only time I've felt grounded is with Warren near. That is scary all on its own.

I look up at him, trying to find the words for what I want to say, but he must not need them. He takes a seat beside me and pulls me into his arms. I cling to him as the tears fall, letting all my sadness and frustration out. I've never cried this much in my life, but here we are again.

"You keep saying that," I mumble against his chest, "but I don't know if I'll ever be okay."

"I know you will, Niccola," Warren replies, and there's no doubt in his voice. "You are the strongest person I've met, and I've met plenty of people. Both young and old. Your spirit will see you through. I have no doubts."

"Well, that makes one of us."

"You're stronger than you give yourself credit for," he says, and I shake my head against his chest.

"You only say that because you like me," I joke, but I can feel his body tense instantly.

"I do like you, Niccola," he whispers, and I know he means it with every part of his soul. I can feel it too. I want to tell him just how much he means to me. I want to accept that I'm never going to be the same. Not without him. But what can we do? Exchange phone numbers and emails when I leave? Because I am leaving. I . . .

"Phone number."

"What?"

I sit up, pushing back from Warren as he looks down at me. There's that nagging thought in my mind again, trying to push through my confusion. He doesn't say anything else, waiting me out as I try to sort myself out.

"Phone number. I remember numbers, and I think it's a phone number."

Warren reaches over and hands me my phone. Carefully, I push all the numbers I can remember into the screen, and when I'm done, it does make up a phone number.

"What is this from?"

"I have no idea. But while I was out, I know I dreamt. Or something. And I remember these numbers. Like they're important."

"Then let's dial."

I glance at him before pushing the button. The phone rings and rings, and after a while, the answering machine picks up.

"Well, at least we know it's a real phone number," Warren says as I disconnect. I stare at the phone, unable to push away the nagging. It feels like I'm missing something. Something big.

"Hey, let's worry about this in the morning." Warren takes the phone out of my hands, and I realize it's two in the morning. I do feel tired, even though I've slept for days. When I move back against the headboard, Warren settles into his chair.

"Could you . . ." I begin, and his eyes fly up to meet mine. That one look gives me the boldness I need to ask the question I want. "Could you stay with me?"

"I am."

"Here." I point to the side of the bed, embarrassment heating up my cheeks. It's so quiet in the room, I feel inclined to hold my breath. But then Warren moves, and the spell is broken. Carefully, he takes a step toward the bed, as I slide down to my back. After another moment, he lies down beside me, a few inches between us. This is the first time I've ever invited a guy into my bed, but I've never felt like I wanted to until this exact moment.

With him beside me, I don't hesitate to relax and let dreamland take me.

Two days go by before I'm feeling better. It's like whatever the sickness was, it drained all my energy. I'm still feeling the effects, but at least I'm back to being outside. Even though this weather is kicking my butt.

Warren sets a cup of coffee in front of me, bringing me out of my thoughts. I've been spending a lot of time at Coffee Haven. Since I ventured outside, all the people I've met have come by to check on me.

It's heartwarming to know how close-knit this community is. The thought also brings sadness, because I know I'll be leaving it soon. As soon as I figure out where to go.

"Hey, what are you thinking about?" Warren asks, gently running his fingers over the top of my hand. Since my sickness, he's been staying close and sleeping beside me every night. We don't touch, and we haven't talked about us in so many words, but I know I scared him.

"I'm thinking that I don't know where to go from here," I reply honestly. I don't want to hide my feelings from him, or from myself. A part of me from before would've put on a brave face. But the part of me from right now just wants someone to share everything with.

"We'll figure this out."

"You keep saying that, but there's nothing more to figure out," I say, but there's no venom in my voice. Just sadness. "It's time for me to move on, to search somewhere else, but I've got nothing. No family to go back to. I'm not sure what waits for me at home."

"You could always stay."

I glance at him sharply, but he's not looking at me. His eyes are on where his hand continues to dance over my skin. There's nothing more I would want than to stay here. But we both know it's just wishful thinking.

I'm not even old enough to be on my own. My savings are running dry. I'll have nowhere to live soon enough. If I'm hoping to find my mother, I'll need to go sooner rather than later. So instead of pouring my heart out to Warren, I turn my hand over and latch on to his.

"Maybe in another life," I whisper, and he looks at me then. There's so much emotion there, it makes my chest hurt. In that moment, the pull I've felt toward him intensifies a hundred times over, and it's all I can do to stay seated. His hand trembles under mine for a moment, and I think he feels it too. We cling to each other as if we're making a promise, but it's a promise neither one of us will be able to keep.

∽

"What do you think you'll do next?" Warren asks, as we walk out of Coffee Haven. There are a lot more people on the street now, tourists coming in for the winter break. It feels unreal to think that there's a whole other world underneath this regular one.

"I think going back to our coven would be the best," I reply reluctantly. It's the last thing I want to do. When I called and checked in with them a week ago, they hadn't even noticed we'd been gone. I guess that's what happens when the rules of close-knit, thirteen-member covens go out the window. Although, maybe it's just the coven back in Palmdale. The one in Havenwood Falls seems to be doing just fine.

"When I spoke to them, they did say I will have a place to stay. And they'll help any way they can."

They're not a bad coven, but they don't feel like mine anymore. Nothing from before Havenwood Falls does.

Warren stays quiet as we walk, and I wonder what he's thinking. We don't seem to have a destination in mind. It's like we both need this time together, as much of it as we can get, while we can.

Suddenly, Warren stops in his tracks, and I turn to face him. He runs his hand over his hair, looking a little awkward all of a sudden.

"Warren?"

"Would you like to go to dinner with me?" he blurts out a little too loud. A few people glance over, with big smiles on their faces, as Warren continues to fidget. Considering we've had almost every meal together for a week, it's strange for him to be nervous. But then I realize he's asking me on a date.

"Yes," I reply without hesitation. His grin blinds me for a second, then he steps closer and tentatively reaches for my hand, as if giving me a choice to pull away. Instead, I meet him halfway, twining our hands together. Sure, we've held hands before, but this feels different. It feels like a beginning.

His phone rings then, and he shrugs apologetically before reaching for it. I take a step away from him to give him some privacy, but he tugs me to stay close. Smiling internally, I tuck myself into his side and wait for him to finish up.

"I can be there in ten minutes," Warren says into the phone, glancing down at me. I nod to let him know it's okay, and we turn to head back to the inn.

After Warren leaves, I sit on the bed, trying to figure out what I'm going to wear. I didn't exactly pack formalwear or anything special. But for Warren, I wanted to dress special. Heading to the bathroom, I stare at myself in the mirror. I don't even recognize myself anymore. It's not just the fact that my hair is silver now, or the fact that I look a little paler than usual. There's a sort of maturity around my eyes that wasn't there before.

I wonder what my mom would think if she saw me now. Would I still look like her little girl or am I a grown woman now? Is there really an age on that or just experience?

As I run my hands over my long locks, a sudden urge almost overtakes me. Marching back into the room, I grab a pair of scissors before walking back over to the mirror. Before I can think too much of it, I take a handful of my hair and cut it right below my collarbone. The weight falls off, and it's like I've been waiting for this. I've wanted to cut my hair this short for years, but Mom always said I'd regret it if it doesn't grow back. Even though my hair grows fast. Now, I'm making this decision for me, and it feels amazing.

I finish cutting my hair in no time at all, and I have to say, I'm a huge fan. I style it the best I can, without any heating tools. I'd love to see it straightened, but that'll have to wait. I go for a more dramatic look with my eye makeup, drawing a thicker and longer cat eye. After a few quick swipes with my mascara, I'm satisfied. I still have nothing to wear, but I decide my black T-shirt and black jeans will look good against the silver hair.

The only thing that's missing now is lipstick. The bright red is my armor, my wall of protection. And right now, it makes me look badass.

I look like the version of myself that I've always seen inside my head. I guess it's true what they say—experiences mold us, in a way nothing else can. I definitely don't feel seventeen anymore. And maybe that's okay.

When the knock on the door comes, I'm ready. I swing the door open to find Warren on the other side, dressed in a dark blue shirt and dark slacks. As cliché as it may be, he takes my breath away. I don't know if anyone else ever will, the way he does. This feels like a magic all on its own.

"You look amazing," he finally says, his eyes roaming over me. "Love the haircut."

I beam at him, every reservation forgotten. The anticipation of tonight has my whole body buzzing. Sure, I've been on dates. But nothing has had me this excited before.

"You ready to go?" Warren asks, and I nod. Walking back into the room, I reach for his jacket, pulling it over my shoulders. It messes with the whole look, since it's so much bigger than I am, but I wouldn't trade it for anything. I turn to see him already grinning at me. If I was a mind reader, I'd guess he likes that I'm still wearing it.

"Let's go," I say.

But before I can take two steps, my phone buzzes, surprising me. I haven't received a phone call in a while. Glancing down, I find the number I called earlier staring back at me. With FaceTime attached to it.

"What is it?" Warren asks, instantly by my side. Turning the phone, I show him the screen.

"Answer it."

I nod and slide the button over. A face comes into the frame, and it makes my head spin.

"Mom."

# CHAPTER 12

"*N*iccola." Her voice sounds exactly how I remember it, but there's a hint of exhaustion on her face that I'm not used to.

"Mom, are you okay? Where are you?"

"What did you do to your hair?"

We talk over each other, then burst out laughing. Seeing her frees me in a whole new way, and I reach for Warren's hand, gripping it tightly. He's still beside me, just out of frame, as I take a seat on the bed.

"I'm so sorry, Nic," my mom says, tears pooling in her eyes. "I never meant for any of this to happen."

"What happened?"

"My past caught up with me."

"I'm going to need more than that, Mom," I say, not pulling any punches. My tone makes her pause, and then she smiles.

"You are so grown up, Nic. I'm sorry for that. I know I pushed you when I disappeared. But it was the only way to keep you safe."

"From what?"

"Some very bad people."

"That's not enough, Mom. This hair? It wasn't by choice. I was sick. A spell did this. I've been worried. I've been left alone with no one to turn to. I need answers, and I need them now."

Warren squeezes my hand in solidarity, and I glance at him for just a moment. But it's enough. Mom sees it.

"Who's there with you?" The alarm in her voice is evident, so I have no choice. I tug Warren into frame.

"This is Warren. He's a deputy. He's been helping me."

"So you've found it."

Warren and I startle at that, sharing another look. She's not making much sense, and I tell her as much.

"Do you remember your grandmother?" Mom asks, instead of answering my question.

"Yeah, she was . . ." But I stop before I get any further, because new images assault me. I'm seven years old, my grandmother and mom are in front of me, arguing about binding my powers. Binding my shifter side. Then they fight, with their magic, to a point where grandmother is banished from our house forever.

"You kicked her out?" I ask, incredulous. Warren glances over at me, but I can't take my eyes off my mother.

"There was a lot you saw as a child that you should've never seen, Nic," Mom replies, regret filling her eyes. "The only good thing your grandmother did was to suppress your memories."

"So, what? I activated a spell that brought them back?"

"You did. It's blood magic, Nic. Wherever you are, something triggered the spell to dissipate it. It's tied heavily to our emotions."

"How did I know to call this number?"

"I made you memorize it when you were little."

My mom exhales visibly, her eyes on mine. Even through the phone screen, I can feel her regret. Her worries over her decisions.

"I'm sorry I left you, Nic," she apologizes once more. "I'm sorry there was no other way. I had to do what I had to do. For both of us."

"What did you do, Mom?"

At first, she doesn't answer. Then she glances to her left, and I realize someone else is there with her. Warren's hand tightens on mine,

79

as if he's making sure I know he's there. And then, *he* steps into the frame.

"Dad?"

"Hello, Nic," my father says, leaning over my mom's shoulder. He looks much like his high school basketball photo, with just a few more years of wear on him. "It's nice to finally talk to you."

"You're . . . what do you mean?" I stumble over my words, trying to find meaning in what I'm seeing and hearing. This is not how I expected the day to go.

"The last time I saw you, you were barely a few years old," my dad says, a small smile on his face that looks much like my own. "I'm sorry I've been gone for so long."

"Please stop apologizing, both of you," I snap, fed up with all of this. Warren trades his hand in mine, putting his right one behind me and rubbing my back a little. I sink into the feeling of him beside me.

"Was Dad one of the things I was meant to forget?" It's taking everything in me not to scream. "I need answers, and I'm done listening to excuses. Why did you both abandon me?"

There are tears in my eyes that I'm not fighting. They've hurt me, in a way a child shouldn't be hurt. I've ignored that this whole time because I wanted to find them. But now that they're in front of me, I won't hide my feelings.

"Oh, Nic," Mom says, reaching towards the screen. "I'm so . . ."

"No. I don't want to hear it."

"We can't tell you everything right now. We're . . ."

The connection freezes for a second, cutting off whatever Mom was going to say.

"Mom?"

The spinning wheel of doom shows up, and I squeeze the phone tighter in my hand.

"We'll explain everything," Mom says, coming back online. "Soon."

Then she reaches over and shuts the call off. Tears spill free as I stare at the black screen, until Warren pulls me into his arms and holds me while I cry all of my frustration out.

~

We stay like that for a while, with Warren holding me tightly, as if with just his arms, he can protect me from the world. But I know I can't stay like this forever, so with great difficulty, I push myself away.

"What now?" I ask, wiping my tears away. I'm sure I look like a mess, most of my makeup smeared down my face. But I can't bring myself to get up, to move away from him. He's holding my hands in his, and it's the only thing keeping me from spiraling.

"I wish I could tell you, Nic," he replies, his voice coated with emotion. "But this is a decision you need to make for yourself."

"I know."

In that moment, I wish for my magic. I can feel it in my blood, in every breath, but I wish I could just let it all out. Send the wind spinning, just so I know I can do something right.

"I'll be leaving in the morning," I announce, coming to a decision right then and there. There's no point in prolonging this, and now that I know my parents are alive, maybe our coven can help me track them down. The longer I stay, the more I don't want to go, so I need to rip off the Band-Aid.

Warren doesn't say anything at first, but I can feel the tension radiating off his body. I'm not sure if there's really anything to say. He knows this is what must be done.

"You know, I'm glad I met you, Niccola Knight-Summers," he whispers, and I grin through the tears.

"I kind of like the sound of that."

"It has a nice ring to it."

We sit in silence, both of us trying to figure out what to do or say next. But all I can think of is how much I wish my life was different.

"Some date this turned out to be," I comment, wiping more tears off my cheeks. Warren reaches over, his own hand following suit, as he studies my face carefully.

"I wouldn't trade it for anything," he replies.

I smile, even though my heart is breaking. There's one thing I do want before I leave, and I think that we both owe ourselves this one moment.

"Can I ask you for something?"

"Anything."

"Can you let me see your wolf?"

He stares at me for a long moment, then nods. I've seen his wolf before, but this feels more personal. Something between just the two of us. Two people meeting on the same playing field.

I close my eyes as I let his magic wash over me and then I feel a small pressure on my hand. Looking up, I find his gorgeous wolf in front of me. He's so big, he comes up to my chest. Even in the dim light, his dark fur glows, and his eyes pierce right through me.

I reach over, plunging my hand into the fur, and I swear he sighs the same moment I do. Without hesitation, I let my hands explore over him, memorizing this form, if only for a small time.

"My magic doesn't allow me to shift," I whisper, as if telling him a secret, "but I can light up the sky."

I let it pool in my palm, the energy from within me, and then I throw it up in the air. The whole room brightens with twinkling lights, dancing around the two of us like stars. Warren shifts while I'm still looking at the ceiling, and I feel his hand take mine.

"You are pretty incredible," he says softly, and I meet his eye, my magic twirling over our skin.

"Right back at ya," I reply, and before I lose my nerve, I ask, "How do you keep your clothes within the shift?"

"It was a gift." I can hear the smile in his voice before I even glance at him. "The Hawthornes enchanted the shift before I left as a way to help me. I was lost back then, missing a part of myself. I'm not so lost anymore."

Every nerve in my body is reaching out to him, but I don't know if I will be able to leave if I give in to it now. Warren doesn't push, but I see the desire mirrored in his own eyes. He's leaving it in my hands once again, and I do the only thing I can. I save us both when I let go and move away.

"I'll come by tomorrow morning," Warren says, moving away as my magic disappears. Just like that, we're back to being polite acquaintances. I want to ask him to stay and sleep beside me one last time, but that feels like too much.

So I walk him to the door, and I lock it behind him. I go back to the bed and lie down on it, clutching his coat to my chest, as tears fall down my cheeks.

# CHAPTER 13

"**A**re you sure this is what you want to do?" Sherry asks, as we stand in the lobby of Whisper Falls Inn. The place has become like a home to me, and I'm sad to be leaving it. Warren must've called them, because both Sherry and Cece meet me downstairs in the morning. The sheriff came by earlier to check on me as well.

"Now that I know she's out there—they're both out there," I say, "there's nothing for me here."

"Are you certain of that?" Cece asks, just as Warren walks through the doors. My eyes catch on his, and no, I'm not certain. But it is what I must do. It doesn't matter how I feel, or what I want. I turn to the angel, tears pooling in my eyes.

"Thank you for your kindness," I say, and Cece pulls me into her arms. Her warmth envelops me, and I cling to her for a moment longer. Then Sherry is there, pulling me into a hug, and I feel like my heart is shattering right here, in front of them.

"I wouldn't have survived without you two," I say, because even though our friendship is brief, I feel like they're the older sisters I've always wished I had. But also the motherly encouragement I needed. I wish I could say I would never forget them, and a part of me thinks I won't. I'll carry their kindness in my heart forever, even if my memories are gone.

"If the winds ever carry you this way, I hope you find us," Cece comments softly, before she and Sherry leave. Each of them give Warren a look, and then they're gone.

"Well, deputy in training," I begin, my whole body buzzing with heartbreak. "I say you've nailed this assignment. Will that earn you your merit badge?"

"I think I might have a chance of adding one to my sash." He smiles, but it doesn't reach his eyes. We both know we're just prolonging the inevitable. But I still can't make myself move. I want to hold onto this moment for as long as I can, even though I won't remember it soon.

"What will you do when you find them?"

I'm grateful he says *when* and not *if*. I need all the confidence I can get right now.

"Demand answers. Maybe yell at them a little and be a typical angsty teenager."

Warren chuckles, and once again, I grab that sound and tuck it into my heart. Maybe I'm being an angsty teenager right now. Maybe I'm being melodramatic. But this right here, it's all I ever wanted, and I want to be selfish and stay.

Taking a deep breath, I walk toward him, knowing that if I don't do this now, I won't be able to do it later. Warren accepts it, and for a second, I wish he didn't. The romantic side of me that I try so hard to repress wants him to fight for me. Wants that epic movie moment where the guy won't let the girl go. But the mature side of me knows that what he's doing, supporting me in this quest of mine, is more important. We're both acting in the best interest of the other, and what is more romantic than that?

The shuttle for the airport sits outside, and the same kind man who drove me here is standing by the open passenger door. Warren and I take our time walking over, not touching, but staying close enough to each other that I can feel his body heat. I'm still wearing his coat, and when we finally stop by the van, I go to shrug it off. His hand lands on my upper arm, halting the process.

"Keep it," he whispers, looking me straight in the eye for the first time this morning. "It'll keep you warm."

And just like that, I'm a puddle of mush, and I reach for him, just as he reaches for me. His arms pull me close, and I tuck myself into him as if I've been custom made for this exact spot. We stand like that, the only two people in the world. A witch and a shifter. Holding on to each other as if our lives depend on it.

"I wish . . ." Warren begins, but I shake my head into his chest. I can't allow him to give me the words, because when I forget them, he won't. This whole time, he hasn't just been protecting me. I've been protecting him. It's why, no matter how much I want to, I can't let myself be selfish and kiss him. I can't let him carry that within his memory, when I won't.

"You're a great deputy, Warren Nichols. You will serve this town well."

"And you, Niccola Knight-Summers, are the most amazing person I have ever met, and you will have a wonderful life."

Tears stain his sweater, but I don't try to hide them. Or how much my heart is breaking. Before either of us can say anything else, I'm pulling away and rushing to the van. Without a look at Warren, I tuck myself in between the seats, my body shaking with silent tears. The driver doesn't question me. But I can feel his eyes in the mirror as he gets behind the wheel. I keep my eyes downcast, until I can't any more. As we pull away, I twist in my seat, my gaze finding Warren. My heart pounds with an intensity that makes my chest hurt as I watch the first guy I've ever loved grow smaller and smaller in the rearview window.

When we pull up to the airport terminal entrance, I feel like I'm coming out of a fog. Tugging my backpack over my shoulder, I pull the coat close to my body as I get out of the van. The movement makes me pause, and I glance down at said coat with confusion. My memory is fuzzy, and I can't quite remember where I got it, but it seems important. My phone dings with a reminder, and I glance down at my ticket.

Something happened, something monumental, but I can't seem to place my finger on it. I glance around, but nothing seems to stand out. Shrugging, I head into the airport. Clearly, Colorado was a bust.

When it's time for my flight, I'm asleep as soon as I sit down in my seat. Exhaustion coats my bones and weighs down my mind. I feel different somehow, but without recalling what happened to me, I can't begin to guess.

The flight doesn't take long, and when I wake up, it's like I haven't rested at all. There was something in my dream, though—a jasmine branch—and I reach for my wrist, almost expecting to see it tattooed there. But there's nothing.

It's like I'm walking through water, just moving from point A to point B, with no coherent plan. I know I bought a ticket, and when I get off the plane, I'm back in my hometown. I know I found out something about my mother, but I can't remember what. I've never felt so lost in my life. By the time I reach our apartment, my face is stained with silent tears and my head is full of pain.

I don't hesitate to lock the door behind me and go straight to my room and my bed, ignoring the mess that still clutters the floor. Lying down, I pull the coat closer to my body, soaking up the comfort it offers, and close my eyes. The tears continue to fall, and for the first time for as long as I can remember, I don't hide from my emotions. I let myself feel it all.

Sometime later, a noise wakes me. I'm not sure how long I've been in this weird semiconscious state, but something pulls me out of it. Carefully, I get off the bed, my battle magic at the ready. It feels good to have it rush through my body, as if I'd been holding myself back before. When I creep over to the partially shut door, I see the shape of a large body in the moonlight. Without hesitation, I step into the living room with a shout.

"Hey!"

The person turns, and my battle magic flies out as a shield around

VALIA LIND

him. But before I can completely disarm him, my mother is there, waving her arms.

"Nic, it's us!"

I drop my hand, relief washing over me like a big wave.

"Mom!"

We rush to each other, and she hugs me close, holding me up in the process because it feels like every ounce of energy I had has gone out of my body. I shudder against her, and more tears leak through my tightly shut lids.

"I'm so sorry, Nic," Mom mumbles against my hair, rubbing my back gently. "I'm so sorry I left you to deal with all this. I'm sorry I kept things from you. I'm so sorry."

"It's okay," I say, pulling back. "You're here now. And you're not alone?"

I haven't forgotten about the man standing at my mom's back. Glancing at him now, I realize he looks a little familiar. He's watching me carefully, as if afraid I'll get spooked again.

"Oh, Nic. This man . . . this is your father."

Shock chills me to the bone as I stare at the person I've never met before, the one I've fantasized about for most of my life. What would it be like to meet him? What would I feel if he suddenly showed up? I thought all I'd feel is joy. But right now, I'm full of questions and caution. Whatever happened changed me. Made me more grown up than my teenage years. And I hold on to that now.

"I think . . ." I glance between my mom and this stranger. "You'd better explain yourselves."

And that's what they do.

88

# CHAPTER 14

"*W*hen your father and I met, we were both running from something. Your grandmother forbade the two of us to be together, and I never understood that, because she wouldn't explain."

"But you got together anyway."

"Love is the most powerful of magics, Nic," the man who is my father speaks up, his eyes intensely on mine. "It breaks through our own spells and rules. I loved your mother the moment I saw her in that parking lot."

"I don't believe in love at first sight," I say, and for some reason, it doesn't taste as true as it used to.

"Do you believe in soul mates?"

The question makes me pause, because a few weeks ago my answer would've been a complete no. But now, something stops me, and I don't understand it.

"That's what I thought," my father says with a knowing smile. "When two people, magic or otherwise, are meant to be together, the rules fly out the window. It's what brought us together," he continues, glancing at my mom. "It's what kept us going all these years."

"But why send me to find my father?" I exclaim, throwing my hands up in the air, "if you knew where he was?"

"I never knew where he was. He left to keep us safe. I had to lead the danger away from our doorstep, and I knew that if anything happened to me, he would be the only person to help you."

"Safe from what?" I stand up, needing to pace, to dispel some of this nervous energy rushing through me.

"From the reason why I had to leave in the first place."

I turn to my father then, picking up on the regret he's feeling, but I'm still not ready to forgive him.

"Explain."

"I come from a very prominent pack," he begins, his gaze on me unwavering. "My father, the alpha, did something that caused a huge fallout, way before I was in the picture. It's too complicated to get into now, and even I don't know the whole story. All I know is that blood must be spilled as repayment—my blood. He thought we would be safe, but we weren't. He sent me away when I was younger, to train, to keep me safe. But as I grew older, the past caught up to me. I'd been on the run for years, and then I met your mother. I thought we could be safe together. But after you were born, you were taken."

"What?" I freeze in my tracks.

"Those who wanted to harm my pack found us and took you, until I promised to return with them. It wasn't a hard choice, Niccola. I gave you up—I gave you both up—to keep you safe. And I would do it all over again."

I didn't think I could feel anything more for this man, but he's shattering my every expectation. I glance at my mother and find her crying silently. It must've broken her, but she pulled herself together and she raised me on her own. All of her lessons, all of her instructions now made sense. She was training me to take care of myself.

"They didn't know then what a powerful witch you would become," my father continues, bringing my attention back to him. "Half witch, half shifter. Both sides from powerful clans. You're the one they want now."

"They're after me?"

"It's why we sent you to Colorado. We've been working on

hunting these supes down, but it'll take time. And you needed to be as far away from us as possible."

With that, I turn away, walking over to the window. Everything they're saying makes sense, but it still doesn't bring back my memories. All I remember is a small pretty town. And some skiing tourists. But I can't bring up anything else. I feel like I'm missing a vital part of myself, and I have no idea why. Taking a deep breath, I turn back to my parents.

"So what now?"

"Now"—my mother stands, walking over to stand in front of me, as she takes both of my hands in hers—"now you go back."

"What? What do you mean?"

"Wherever you were, you were safe. We couldn't even find you. That means you'll be safe there. We're close, Nic. We're close to figuring this out. You need a home. A place you can finish growing up, in safety I can no longer provide you."

"Mom, you can't be serious. Let me help you!"

"This is our fight," Mom says, running her hand over my face. "Yours will come sooner than you think. But I need you to be a kid for a little longer and let us handle this."

"I don't want to. Not when I just got you back." I've never sounded so young, even to my own ears.

"We're never too far away, honey," my mom says, pulling me into her arms once more. After a moment, we both turn to my father, and he stands in one fluid motion before he hugs us both.

I hold on to my parents, hold on to the truths they told me. The sacrifices they made. And I vow to myself that I will always be the best person I can be. I will make them proud.

Five days later, my mother and I are standing on the side of the road next to a rental car in Colorado. I spent three glorious days with my parents, getting to know my dad and both of them as a couple. But then real life set in, and he took off to give Mom a chance to bring me back to Colorado. We took quite a few precautions, flying to places nowhere near here, and cloaking ourselves in half a dozen spells. Now we're in a truck stop in Durango. Without knowing where we're going or what we're looking for, Mom and I decided to drive around to see if we can find whatever we need.

Just as Mom heads back to the car, a van pulls up that looks vaguely familiar. It's the same type of van I got out of at the airport.

"Mom!" I exclaim, feeling a pull toward the pictures on the vehicle.

"What is it?"

"I think—I think we should follow that bus."

She watches me for a tense moment, then glances at the van and the people piling in. Without hesitation, she nods, and we get into the rental.

The drive is twisty, but Mom keeps up with the van well enough. The closer we are to the shuttle, the more determined I feel that this is a sign. That we need to be here. When we pass the *Welcome* sign, it flashes in my memory, but I still can't place where I've seen it before.

Main Street spreads out in front of us, and we pull up a few spaces away from where the van parks. For a moment, I can't seem to move. Everything about this place calls to me, and I don't understand it.

My mom gasps, and I turn to her instantly. I find her eyes are full of tears, and I reach for her, alarmed.

"Mom?"

"Oh my, I remember this place."

"I don't understand." I wait for her to explain, but she just watches the street through the windshield, tears running down her face.

"It's okay, honey," she says, patting my hand. "You will."

She gets out of the car, reaching for her phone. I have no idea who she's calling, but she walks off far enough that I can't hear what's being said. I stand on the side of the street, watching the town, fascinated by all the holiday decorations and snow. I don't think I've ever seen so much snow in my life. Again, something prickles the back of my mind, but I can't quite place it.

"We're all set," Mom says, coming up to stand beside me. She takes my hand, gripping it tightly, and I want to ask her what's going on.

But then a dark blue Toyota 4Runner pulls to the side of the road, and a door opens. Mom and I turn, hand in hand, as a body steps out.

"Hello, Ms. Summers," the man speaks, still covered by the light of the headlights. "I've been sent to retrieve Nic . . . Niccola."

I don't miss the way his voice catches or the familiarity with which he speaks my name. My mom greets him in return as he steps around the vehicle. Gorgeous, like the break of dawn, the guy can't be but a few years older than me. His dark blue eyes meet mine, and in that moment, my whole world rights itself.

It becomes hard to breathe as images assault me, one after the other.

His smile.

His touch.

His reassuring presence.

My mom calls out to me, but it's like I have tunnel vision, and he's the light at the end. I feel a buzzing start in my chest and spread out across my body. I'm hot and elated and completely enthralled by the sight of him.

"Warren," I breathe out finally.

His eyes flash with surprise, quickly overshadowed by desire. We move at the same time; I throw myself at him and he catches me and holds me close. He feels like coming home, and I hope I never have to know what losing him feels like. It's as if all of my limbs are finally properly working again, as if the darkness has lifted.

He sets me down on my feet, gazing down at me in wonder. And something else.

"You remember everything?" he asks, not taking his eyes off me, and I nod.

"You're bonded."

Warren and I turn to my mother, standing just a few feet away with a soft smile on her face.

"Bonded?" I ask, as I reach for Warren's hand and entwine our fingers together. Mom doesn't miss the gesture, nodding her head carefully.

"Remember how your father said there is a magic stronger than ours?"

"Love," I say, blushing as I glance at Warren. "He said love is more powerful."

"And even more so, the soul mate bond."

"But we're not—" I begin, but can't finish. Because Mom's words make sense. The pull I've felt toward him since the moment I met him, the feeling of belonging. The pain of my heart breaking when I drove away. The memories of him returning the moment I set my eyes on him. It happened so fast, but it's the only thing in my life that makes sense like no other.

"We are," Warren says, looking deeply into my eyes.

I want to pull him close and finally find out what he tastes like, but I'm not about to do that in front of my mother. When I turn to her, she steps toward me, opening up her arms.

"Now I can rest easy, knowing you will be not only safe, but loved."

I hold onto her, realizing she must remember this town. Her memory came back faster than mine did.

"You remember?" I ask.

"I do. And I wish I could carry that memory with me. I wish I could share it with your father."

"Maybe one day, you can come back here and you will."

I cling to her, realizing that she'll be leaving and forgetting all about where I am. And I will have no way of reaching her. Dad has made arrangements for finances for me, so I know I'll be taken care of on that front.

"You are a strong, smart, beautiful girl," Mom says, pulling back to look me in the eyes. "You are going to do amazingly well in school, and you will have a good life. Just be brave, Nic. Stay brave."

# CHAPTER 15

The next week goes by in a blur. Mom and Dad are gone who knows where, and they have no idea where I am. The Luna Coven's magic is strong, and my mom no longer remembers where she dropped me off. Or the fact that she knew my dad when they were younger. It'll be up to me to find them when the time is right.

My jasmine tattoo is now a permanent addition to my wrist, and I had Addie add a moon behind it. I don't want to forget that I come from two worlds. My witch and my shifter side are each a part of me, and now I accept them both.

Sherry and Cece have helped me get my apartment in order. I'm now a resident of Havenwood Village, and as weird as it seems to be living on my own, I'm not opposed to it. It feels like the natural next step in my life. And I won't be a child for much longer. My birthday is a little over a month away.

It's funny how things work out sometimes. A month ago I didn't know what I would do with my life. But here I am, getting ready to finish high school at an actual school. Looking for a part time job so I can buy some decorations for my apartment. And going on a first date with a guy I'm completely crazy about.

I look at myself in the mirror, running my hand over my silvery locks. I've come to appreciate my new color. Mom said the spell must've activated my shifter gene. Silver is the color of Dad's wolf. It's kind of cool that I get to carry that part of him with me everywhere I go.

My dress is black and simple. I've got black leggings on underneath, with tall black boots. Getting used to this weather is going to take a while. For some reason, I definitely didn't inherit my dad's shifter temperature regulator. The knock comes as I'm applying my signature red lipstick.

"You look incredible," Warren says the moment I open the door. He's wearing dark slacks and a dark sweater, and he makes my knees buckle. I smile and reach for the coat.

"Didn't you get a warmer coat?" he asks, as I shrug on the coat he gave me. I grin at him, stepping close and twining my hand through his.

"But this one is my favorite."

He grins, leading me out of the apartment and to his truck.

"Where are we going?" I ask, as he opens the door for me. Warren walks around the truck before replying.

"What have you been craving for days?"

"Umm, Chinese food?"

"You got it."

I clap my hands as he turns the car on and chuckles over my enthusiasm. Since this whole ordeal, I have grown a lot as a person. I have learned how to appreciate the smallest things in life. Getting Chinese food when I've been craving it is one of those.

"Sakura Buffet," I read the sign, while Warren parks. "You know, we could've walked."

"And have you become a frozen popsicle? No, thank you."

I laugh as he opens the door for me and takes my hand once more.

"I'm not that bad."

"Maybe. Maybe not," Warren replies, before leaning down and whispering right in my ear. "But I was not taking any chances. This date was not getting cancelled."

Tiny goosebumps race up my spine as his breath washes over my skin. My body heats up to a point where I probably don't need this coat anymore. I match his intensity completely. Between getting myself situated in town and dealing with my parents being gone, we haven't spent any proper time together. But the need in his eyes matches my own, so I tug on his arm before we can walk inside the restaurant.

"Then let's get this date started properly," I say, right before I pull him down to me. His lips crash into mine, and it's as if the whole world has exploded around us.

He tastes like adventure and comfort.

Like desire and friendship.

Like I belong to no one else but him.

I am his, and he is mine.

I have staked my claim, and he has answered in kind.

"Now that's a way to start off a date." Warren grins when we finally come up for air.

"Can't wait to see what comes next," I reply.

Whatever it is, I'm thankful I have found my way to Havenwood Falls.

We hope you enjoyed this story in the Havenwood Falls High series of novellas featuring a variety of supernatural creatures. The series is a collaborative effort by multiple authors. Each author writes a stand-alone story, so you can read them in any order.

Other books in the Young Adult Havenwood Falls High series, in recommended order of reading (however, each author has written a stand-alone story, so they can be read in any order):

*Inamorata* by Randi Cooley Wilson
*Fata Morgana* by E.J. Fechenda
*Forever Emeline* by Katie M. John
*Reclamation* by AnnaLisa Grant
*Avenoir* by Daniele Lanzarotta
*Avenge the Heart* by Michele G. Miller
*Curse the Night* by R.K. Ryals
*Blood & Iron* by Amy Hale
*Shadows & Spells* by Cameo Renae
*Falling Deep* by J.L. Weil
*Saving Infiniti* by Rose Garcia
*Willful* by Liz Ferry
*Cast in Moonlight* by Ali Winters
*Promise the Moon* by Kallie Ross
*Blurred Lines* by Daniele Lanzarotta
*Ascending Darkness* by J.L. Weil
*Finding Infiniti* by Rose Garcia
*Unicorn's Lament* by Megan Linski
*Paper Bird* by Amy Richie
*Rediscovered* by Morgan Wylie

Subscribe to our reader group and receive free stories and more!

# ABOUT THE AUTHOR

*USA Today* bestselling author. Photographer. Artist. Born and raised in St. Petersburg, Russia, Valia Lind has always had a love for the written word. She wrote her first published book on the bathroom floor of her dormitory while procrastinating studying for her college classes. Since graduation, she has moved her writing to more respectable places, and has found her voice in Young Adult fiction. Her YA thriller *Pieces of Revenge* is the recipient of the 2015 Moonbeam Children's Book Award.

AN EXCERPT

*Rediscovered* (A Havenwood Falls High Novella) by Morgan Wylie

**From *USA Today* bestselling author Morgan Wylie comes a new story in the saga of the Havenwood Falls Blackstone witch hunters.**

Brice Blackstone is a black sheep, born with dark hair and the only male ever marked as a witch hunter in Havenwood Falls. He now knows there are others, but as his powers are reawakening, he fears what will happen. After all, the other males are rogues, assassins not only after witches but all supernatural kind. And nobody knows what to expect with him since—as he's heard throughout his whole life—he is different.

His experiences are definitely different. Strange dreams. Voices in his head. The help he secretly accepts from an unlikely source. And then there's the way he reacts to the surprise visitor, opposite of everyone else.

Sunny is an anomaly. Always has been. Dante, leader of the rogue hunters, let her march to her own drum, as she's a valued member of his crew. So when she shows up in Havenwood Falls, Brice's family goes on full alert.

Brice believes in Sunny, though. She knows things nobody else does—like how he can control the witch hunter within before it takes control of him. And in a town full of witches, he must master himself or lose everything he knows and loves.

# REDISCOVERED

## BY MORGAN WYLIE

"Come on, Brice, don't be a baby!" a guy from school taunted from the other side of the fence enclosing the skate park located in Danzan Park. Chadwick Linton was a basketball jock, a witch, and a jerk. Brice ignored him, but a tingling sensation he had never felt before started in the palms of his hands, then moved into his wrists and up his forearms. Brice instinctively flexed his hands and swallowed a gasp. The sensation in his forearms was the telltale sign a witch hunter felt when in a witch's presence.

Could he be transitioning right here, right now? He was almost eighteen, after all, and that was the golden age when the witch hunters from his family tended to come into their own. He knew some of what might happen from his sister Macy's experience when the witch hunter reawakened within her, but he was different. Or so he'd been told all his life. Brice didn't know *all* of what to expect, so he couldn't be sure his transition had begun. He shook his hands out, trying to make the tingles go away, but Chadwick was too close to him.

*Head in the game.* The only way out of there was to skate his way out. Otherwise, he wouldn't outlive the jokes and comments from the other guys. The skateboard world could be tough, even in Havenwood Falls. Either you were a skateboarder or you were a poser. Brice wasn't a poser.

"You've done harder tricks than that. Don't get psyched out!" another guy shouted from the sidelines. Brice recognized all the kids there. Most were classmates he'd known the majority of his life, either from attending Havenwood Falls High School or more recently from the private school, Sun and Moon Academy. Out of the corner of his eye, he noted Jordan Woods hanging out in his football jersey, surrounded by Zoey Mills, Emma Cardin, and Celeste Long, along with the newer guy, Jonathan Burns.

Brice had gone to Havenwood Falls High—the public school—since he was a freshman, but the family, concerned for what might happen when he did transition, pulled Brice out of Havenwood Falls High his senior year and enrolled him in the private school. They gave explicit instructions to the headmaster to not put Brice in any classes with witches. As the witch-to-anything-else ratio at the Academy was higher than at the public school, Brice ended up with a lot of independent study time for his senior year.

His older brother, Brock, who now runs Soothing Sips tasting room in the town square, also attended the public school, so Brice was bummed to be the only one in his family who wouldn't be a Havenwood Falls High graduate. He hated leaving some of his friends, but the truth was he liked the change of pace at the Academy. He had more freedom and independence. Some thought the private school was for troubled kids who couldn't control their magic—and maybe that was the case—but others attended whose parents wanted to keep their kids more exclusive to the supernatural sector.

Brice's friend Samuel Milton, who didn't ride a skateboard, stood behind him with a few others, including Cade Peters, a hellhound a couple years younger from his new school. Dalton Underwood, a Havenwood Falls High sophomore, stood nearby with his board, waiting his turn. They had set up a bit of a practice competition and invited a bunch of people to come out and watch. For the middle of October, it was an unusually pleasant afternoon, and all the kids wanted to be outside after school.

Samuel playfully punched the back of Brice's bicep.

"Don't listen to 'em, Brice. Don't do it if you don't feel it," he encouraged with whispered vigor. Samuel Milton still attended HFH, and Brice had missed hanging out with him every day. Samuel was a lynx shifter and also Macy's best friend Ruby Jean's little brother, so they had practically grown up together. But Samuel didn't understand the skateboarding culture, nor the pressure to perform in a way to prove legitimacy.

Brice cringed inside, knowing the other guys would make fun of him if they heard Samuel attempting to help him back out. The last thing Brice wanted was to back out. He knew he could make the run; it was a standard drop into the bowl, maneuver some tricks, then make his way through the half pipe and finally complete the course with tricks on the rails. But something inside him held him back.

And that made him mad.

Brice wasn't a chicken. He was a good skateboarder, one of the best in Havenwood Falls, in fact. Quickly he glanced all around him to ensure nothing littered the ramps. While doing so, he noticed the Blaekthorn twins—wolf shifters, Weston and Drake—standing nearby, as well as other kids, including Gianna Augustine and Aurelia Petran. Another girl named Ellie Lewis stood by, which made him smile. She'd had a rough past couple years losing her brother, and he hadn't seen her much.

Halloween was quickly approaching, and in Havenwood Falls, even the playground got decorated. He chuckled internally, then got back to business. If he didn't make the drop soon, his spot would be taken by another rider, and he'd be out of the competition, forever seen as a coward.

"I'm going!" he announced, swiping the floppy dark hair from his forehead and taking a deep breath. *Piece of cake.*

Brice jumped on his custom-designed skateboard, dropped into the bowl just deep and wide enough to gain momentum before attempting to stall at the top edge rail, then back down into the depths of the bowl for another round. Once out of the bowl, he did a kick turn and flew down the ramp, dropping into the lower half-pipe, gaining speed as he went. From there he'd complete the course with kick turns and tricks from grinding the axle of his board on the rails to grabbing his board in the air for a 180 turn. He had visualized this moment over and over again. It was a no-brainer in his mind.

His mom would freak if she knew he didn't wear his helmet, but he never did and neither did the other "real" skateboarders. It was one less thing they could make fun of him for. It wasn't like he really cared what they thought, but he didn't want to be *that* guy—the one who always obeyed the rules, the one who always listened to his mommy, the one who still answered to his parents. He wasn't a rebel by a long shot, but he still had moments where he felt like he wanted to be one.

His mom rode his ass like no one else in his family. She was overbearing and treated him like a baby. Lilith Blackstone might sit on the Court of the Sun and the Moon, but she didn't need to dictate his life. After all, he was going to be eighteen soon, and then he could move out and live his own life just like Macy had wanted to, except this time he was prepared for his hunter awakening—at least as much as he could be, being the only male witch hunter in Havenwood Falls.

After Macy had left Havenwood Falls a few years ago, afraid of what her hunter side would become, she made sure her family told Brice everything he needed to know. Brice appreciated that she cared so much, but he didn't understand what the big deal was anyhow or why they made it an event to awaken the hunter. From Macy's stories, he knew the rogue Blackstone witch hunters had other males, and their gifts weren't suppressed early on. They grew up knowing all about themselves and their talents and what they could do. Brice didn't want to be a witch hunter in the sense the rogues were, but he didn't understand why his family made it such a big deal in Havenwood Falls.

Brice made several smaller jumps and did some tricks along the way as he gained speed and confidence leading up to the big jumps at the end. He heard a group cheering off to the side. He turned his head and gave the ladies on the sideline a tip of his head. He should focus but wanted to be the cocky jock type just for a moment. But when he looked, he caught only one set of eyes in the crowd. Bright blue ones surrounded by light golden-blond hair.

He knew those eyes—witch hunter eyes—though he didn't know

who they belonged to. His vision tunneled as his eyes locked onto hers. Electrical shocks sizzled across the back of his neck. Definitely a hunter, one he didn't know.

Brice flew through the air. The ground went out from underneath him. The girl made him feel weightless like he could fly. Or perhaps he was flying.

Her blue eyes went wide, and her face paled more than it already was.

"BRICE!" several voices screamed from somewhere in the distance. Brice couldn't understand what was happening. He felt like everything moved in slow motion. Life had suddenly become crystal clear. He wanted to be free to be all he could be. All the bottled up potential he felt brewing inside him was ready. This was his time. His body tickled with energy surging through from his head down to his toes. Tingles shot up and down his arms. Witches were near. He had never fully felt them before. Maybe he would finally discover the kind of hunter he would become. Maybe this was his awakening.

Instant pain replaced euphoric energy.

"Dude! You flew!" said a voice Brice recognized but couldn't put a name to.

"Are you messed up, bro?" a rather hesitant male voice asked. "What were you doing?"

"Brice, can you hear me?" an unfamiliar female voice called as if she pushed her way through to him with those bright blue eyes.

"Brice, are you all right?" a separate male voice said, filled with panic.

"Keep him still. I called the clinic." That had to be Ellie Lewis. Her stepfather was a doctor at the clinic.

"And I called his mom," a voice—Samuel—offered. Of course Samuel called his mom. He was going to be in so much shit, but until the pain subsided, he wasn't sure he really cared.

Then darkness replaced the pain, and he felt no more.

Purchase *Rediscovered* where books are sold.

www.ingramcontent.com/pod-product-compliance
Lightning Source LLC
Chambersburg PA
CBHW020417130626
46549CB00006B/2603